C0-AQZ-261

DESIRE PROVOKED

Tracy Daugherty

DESIRE PROVOKED

RANDOM HOUSE NEW YORK

 Published in the United States by Random House, Inc., New York and simultaneously in Canada by Random House of Canada Limited, Toronto

Grateful acknowledgment is made to the following for permission to reprint previously published material:

Laurie Anderson: Excerpt from "Let X = X"/It Tango, words and music by Laurie Anderson. Copyright © 1982 by Difficult Music. Reprinted by permission.
Little, Brown and Company: Poem #378 from *The Complete Poems of Emily Dickinson*, edited by Thomas H. Johnson. Copyright 1935 by Martha Dickinson Bianchi. Copyright renewed 1963 by Mary L. Hampson. Reprinted by permission.

Library of Congress Cataloging-in-Publication Data

Daugherty, Tracy.
Desire provoked.

I. Title.
PS3554.A85D4 1986 813'.54 86-11847
ISBN 0-394-55334-9

Manufactured in the United States of America

98765432

FIRST EDITION

Book design by Carole Lowenstein

For my family

Part One

CARTER, Adams' boss, has developed a lively system for recognizing merit. Some years ago he returned from a holiday in South America with several insects in a box. They had been treated with a mixture of South American tree saps and preserved in cotton. Though they resembled common tree roaches, these were, Carter assured his associates, intelligent creatures: *platula*, a species domesticated for over five centuries by the Indians. Native to Peruvian rain forests, the bugs were originally attracted to the aroma of the Indians' pipes. They would crawl onto smokers' shoulders and perch there like parakeets. "The relationship of certain South American Indians and their insects parallels that of the American Indian and his dog," Carter said. When a favorite insect died, it was coated with tree sap and worn around the neck on a string.

Carter bronzed the bugs and made them into pins. He decided to collect insects wherever he went: *Carausius morosus* from Asia, *Bellicostermes* from

Africa, *Glossina* from Saudi Arabia. He had them dipped in bronze, silver, and gold, like Olympic medals, and distributed them to his employees as merit badges. A five-year man received a bronze *Dolichorespula saxonia.* Ten years earned a silver *Polistes bimaculatus.* The *Buthus*, Orb spider, and *Ixodes ricinus* were bonus pins.

At first the employees of On-Line Information Systems reacted with distaste, but when it became apparent that Carter set store by the bugs, the pins gained value within the corporate structure.

Adams has more bugs than his peers. At work he wears the *Ixodes* on his lapel. Before leaving the office at night he carefully removes it from his coat and drops it in his pocket.

"Some decisions, Sam, I need to make without you," his wife insists. Pamela is beautifully pale, Pennsylvania Dutch, a strict guardian of her youthful health and happiness. Her father, a Lutheran minister, told her nightly end-of-the-world stories when he tucked her into bed; she's fond of overstatement. Often she refers to the topography of her body, the scale of her emotions, and the basin of depression in which Adams has placed her.

Last week, in a long-meditated move, she left with the kids and their fabulous toys.

"An investor and a father, who am I to say whether running from our wives is the problem, a result of the problem, or a symptom of some larger ill," Adams writes his younger brother. Kenny is a session drummer in Burbank. "All I know is, we are collectively bored, we're not in love—we're no longer interested, here, in the pretense of love. Whether this makes us more or less civilized than other men is not for me to say.

"Our wives' reactions have been standard. They claim that our defections are standard. In a way, our behavior has been entirely predictable. The violence of our daughters, of course, is something none of us could've foreseen.

"One positive note: to combat boredom we've spent an inordinate amount of time on the job. Some marvelous work has resulted. The artists among us have been particularly successful. Last night in the town square a local acting troupe presented a charming skit, 'The Return of the Black Death,' in costumes entirely fashioned out of cereal boxes."

Within days of moving into the new house with their mother, the kids have accidents. First a hot-water heater in the pantry ruptures, a small hole at the bottom scalding Toby's calf. Then Deidre burns her eyebrows lighting the oven. "I was teaching her to help me in the kitchen," Pamela tells Adams. "I didn't know she'd already turned on the gas."

Sometimes after sunset boys light fireworks in the field behind his house. Rockets glide through the grass. The boys scatter when Adams comes to the window, though he doesn't mean to frighten them. He remembers the field he played in as a kid (Red Cloud, Nebraska, geographical center of the nation, latitude forty degrees) and enjoys the fragmenting colors. On cool evenings, as the frogs chirp, he stands with a glass of Scotch at the screen door, imagining the miles between his home here in Elgin and the house where he was born. He has never mapped that particular stretch of Nebraska—faded Indian trails, mistletoe high in the trees, a thin pitted blacktop.

Tonight, an unusually warm night in March, he is naked in the dark. He pours himself a Scotch, then opens a package of Rainbo Rolls. From the kitchen window he glimpses a man in a dark blue suit standing in the shadows at the gate. Looking closely, Adams believes it to be young Jordan from the Records Office. Tall, blond, large head and hands. Pamela once remarked at a party that Jordan would be a nice-looking man if he'd cut his hair.

What is he doing in Adams' backyard?

Adams buckles his pants and steps outside. A heavy mist is falling. Hair prickles on his chest. He is not at all sure, now, that this man is Jordan. Too much paunch.

"Who's there?" he calls, switching on the outside light. "Who is it?" In the time it takes his eyes to adjust to the glare the man is gone. Adams, barefooted, steps onto the grass, touching the barbecue pit as he pauses to look around. Charcoal blackens his fingers. His feet are cold. He returns to the house, straightens the half-finished map on his table, and picks up a pen. Sketching farm roads and freeways has always helped him calm down.

Pamela phones. "I told my parents, Sam. There didn't seem to be any sense keeping it a secret any longer."

"How'd they take it?"

"They were shocked, naturally. Wanted to blame you for everything. I told them that wasn't fair."

"Thank you."

"I tried, Sam, God knows I tried. Didn't I try, Sam?"

"Yes. What can I say?"

Pamela hangs up.

He turns on the television. Lee Trevino misses a putt. Adams turns it off. He walks into the bathroom, smooths the top of his head in the mirror. He is fair-skinned, with slightly reddish-brown hair. Small shoulders.

He calls Pamela back. "Why don't you stop this and come home?" he says.

"I was thinking of talking to a lawyer."

"What about?"

"Irreconcilable differences."

"The only difference is you're lost and I'm not." Immediately he apologizes, to keep her on the line. He mentions the stranger in his yard.

"Can you pick Deidre up at dance class?"

"All right."

At six he drops by the studio. Deidre's flushed from the workout, her hair is damp.

"How's my room," she asks.

"Just as you left it."

"Good." She's eight years old and thinks she's on vacation. His son, Toby, who is twelve, seems to have grasped matters, though he's been temperamental since he was ten and doesn't offer his thoughts.

Deidre is silent for two blocks. Then: "I want everything to be perfect."

"How do you mean?"

"You know."

"Tell me."

"When I come back."

"Ah." What has Pamela promised? "Does your mother say you'll be coming back soon?"

Deidre doesn't answer.

"Well," Adams says, rubbing the back of her neck. "Everything *will* be perfect. We'll see to it."

"Daddy, what do you do?"

"What do I do?"

"At home. By yourself."

"Oh. Well. Let's see. I watch television."

"Good," she says. "That's good."

They have a night-light in the shape of a bear. It gives them strength—he hears it in their voices when they call. They roar on the telephone, fraying the lines between their mother's house and his, over stretches of debits and credits. When he drives past their house at night, the porch light sears him to the bone. His tires go bald. He belongs on the other side of that light, a scarecrow guarding his children's sleep. At home he replaces a burnt-out kitchen bulb. It illuminates things no longer there: a safe-deposit box, a bottle of Old Charter, a gold dish where Pamela placed her rings before washing the plates after dinner.

Their first child, Alan, died in the hospital after three hard days. He was premature, small as a shoe. Adams stood at the nursery window urging his son to hold on, but the little lungs couldn't do it, Alan turned blue, the nurses wheeled him away. Adams sat in an old green chair in the waiting room, no longer a father. *Leave It to Beaver* played on a Magnavox TV on a shelf near the ceiling.

Pamela closed her eyes when Adams told her about the baby. The birth had been difficult and she was still exhausted. The room was yellow, square, pungent with alcohol and talcum. The sun was taking a long time to set and Adams was hot in his long-sleeved shirt, his face felt oily. He kissed Pamela's fingers, she stroked the soft skin above his lip. "It's okay," he whispered into her hand.

Later, once she was asleep, Adams rode the elevator. He paced each floor of the hospital, one after the other.

Families waited on their doctors. Nurses came and wheeled people away.

Pavarotti is singing "E lucevan le stelle" from *Tosca.* The large mole on the left side of his face somehow looks attractive, riding the crook of his beard. In his right hand he holds a white handkerchief; so far he has done nothing with it. When he raises his head, eyes brimming with tears, Adams is moved, but his attention is continually drawn to either the handkerchief or the mole.

Meanwhile, the chicken breasts on Adams' cutting board are drying out. They've been there since five, when he turned on the television. He goes into the kitchen, pulls chili powder and cumin from the spice rack, then spreads parsley in the bottom of a dish to make a bed for the chicken. He butters the chicken and lays the pieces in a pleasant pattern on the parsley.

Pamela seems to have taken the cilantro.

Returning to the living room, he is in time to see Pavarotti bow. The handkerchief swings from his fingers.

Someone taps on Adams' door. It's the Reverend Sister Rosa, a fortune-teller from down the block. "Hi," she says, adjusting a thin black shawl on her shoulders. "I wanted everyone in the neighborhood to know I'm giving a group discount on Tarot readings. Wednesday nights. If you come with a friend, it's half off for you and free for the friend. I'll also have complimentary cheese and coffee."

"Thanks very much," Adams says. "But I have a standing engagement on Wednesday nights. I play at a little dance club."

"Oh, well, too bad." Rosa sniffs. "You've just sprayed your house? I need to spray mine."

"That's the chicken," Adams says.

She gives him a curious look. "I miss those little munchkins of yours. Haven't seen them lately."

"My wife left a couple of weeks ago. The kids are staying with her."

"Vacation?"

"No, we separated."

"I'm sorry to hear it." She fumbles with her shawl. "You know, I could give you a private reading anytime you'd like. Find out when you'll be lucky in love."

"Thanks. I'll keep that in mind."

"See you."

"Good-bye."

She walks next door and rings the doorbell.

Adams removes the chicken from the oven, wraps it in foil, and places it in the refrigerator.

Pete and Denny have worked up a new song—Otis Redding's "Sittin' on the Dock of the Bay." They are teaching Bob the chords when Adams arrives. Adams sets up, fills in a standard beat, then adds a few flourishes as he becomes familiar with the breaks. He is still sore from helping Pamela move.

Denny, their lead vocalist, is no King of Soul but he's funky, and Bob decides to include the new song in the final set.

Morty's Place is crowded on Wednesdays because Morty serves beer and wine to minors between ten and midnight. "Only on Wednesdays, and only if you're as discreet about it as I am," he tells the teenagers. He's on good terms with the sheriff and in no danger of losing his license. The band begins at nine. Other bands play throughout the week, so Adams has to store his drums in a back room.

Together he and Kenny wore out three copies of Lloyd Price's "Lawdy Miss Clawdy," featuring rockin' sockin' Earl Palmer, when they were young. They played along with the record after school almost every day. Kenny had magic in his wrists. He taped their mother's Kotex to his tom-toms to get the sound he wanted. Adams played for enjoyment.

The songs become routine after a while, guitarists and vocalists get the spotlight—it's the positioning of the drums on stage, the tightening of the wing nuts, the tuning, the *anticipation* that gives him the pleasant edge he needs to perform well. He adjusts the ride cymbals, tightens his snare, loosens the head on the floor tom. Temperature variations inevitably cause the drums to slip out of tune, and he spends a solid hour tapping the tight heads, ears close to his fingers, searching for the right sounds with the drum key. He lays three extra pairs of sticks, 9A (thin), beside the bass drum. Brushes and soft mallets he keeps on an old music stand behind his leather stool, known in the trade as a drummer's throne.

The drums sparkle dark blue. He bought the set two years ago with extra money he earned mapping the sea floor off Japan. It was his last international assignment.

Bob, the bassist, sells Lincoln-Mercuries. He is Adams' dealer. Through him, Adams met the other members of the band: Pete, a radio newsman who idolizes Les Paul, and Denny, a local jeweler who likes to flash his rings while sawing on rhythm guitar. For a year they practiced in Bob's basement; then, billing themselves simply as the "Bob Parke Combo," auditioned for Morty. In those days Adams still had his first set, which he'd put together over a period of years, buying used drums whenever he could afford them: A Ludwig snare, a Slingerland bass drum, a Gretsch tom-tom. With the purchase of his first Zildjian cymbal, the top of the line, he felt versatile and whole.

Pamela had infinite patience with his music when they first started dating at the University of Nebraska. At the time he was trying to make an Indian tom-tom from aspen wood and cowhide. In studying ancient maps he had run across Chippewa drums, whose heads were painted to represent the world. On his strip of cowhide he drew a pattern in which the edge represented the ocean, the bisecting lines the fields of the

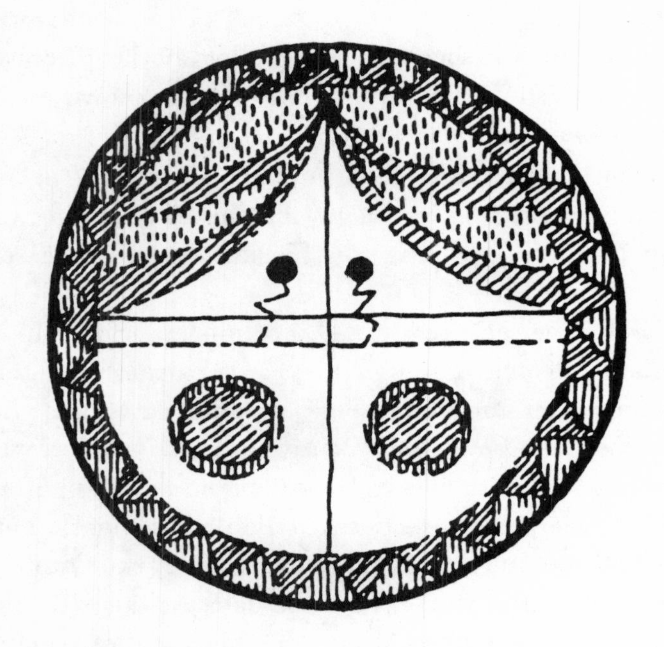

earth, the drapery a battery of storm clouds, the jagged lines lightning, and the spots below thunder. It was one of his earliest maps.

For the Chippewa, the drum had the power of both thunder and the heartbeat. For Adams, it held only frustration; he was unable to carve the wood to his liking. Pamela tried to help, but was no more skilled than he. At night he played with a jazz trio at a coffee house near campus. Each weekend Pamela came to listen, ordering cup after cup of cappuccino. The same songs every Saturday, but she never seemed to sour.

They tune for twenty minutes, order drinks, then with a kickbeat Adams propels them into the blues. Soon they are galloping to Merle Haggard—Bob does a "cowboy shift" in the middle of the song, from C to C sharp, signaling Adams he wants to run with this awhile, and they jam for fifteen minutes. By this time the club is packed—middle-aged men, mostly, still in their business suits, though a number of teenaged girls twist around the dance floor.

Some nights Adams leaves the club exhausted. On other nights he doesn't want to stop. There's no accounting for it. Whether the band is up or not has nothing to do with his own physical reaction to the music. He can feel bored when they're playing well, excited when they're sloppy. Tonight, when the final set ends, just after two, he's wide awake, hungry, talkative. So is Pete, so they go for breakfast at Adele's, an all-night diner.

"I'll be shit on the air tomorrow," Pete says. He has a six A.M. news broadcast. "Every morning it's Nicaragua, Nicaragua. I can't even *say* Nicaragua till about noon."

Adams orders orange juice and pancakes. He remembers the chicken in his refrigerator. At three o'clock, when he finally reaches home, Jordan is standing in his yard. Adams calls the police. "I'm sorry, sir," the sergeant says. "You're out of our jurisdiction."

Adams argues that his neighborhood is well within

the city limits. The sergeant insists that county records are unclear. By now the man has disappeared.

Deidre answers the door and leaps into his arms, her hands gummy with peach ice cream. "Can we go to a movie, Daddy?"

"If you want to," he says, kissing her sticky cheek.

Pamela is dressed to go out. "There's an opening tonight at Cyndi's gallery," she says. "She may be interested in showing my photographs. A friend's picking me up."

Adams does not mistake the tone of her voice. She's seeing a man. As if unsure of his footing, he walks slowly back to the car holding Deidre in his arms.

He treats the kids to hamburgers and *Raiders of the Lost Ark*. At home, he clears dirty dishes from the coffee table and newspapers from the couch so they can watch TV. He brings them milk.

"Daddy, how old are you?" Deidre asks.

"Forty-one."

"Is that old?"

"Not too."

"Are you older than Mom?"

"She's thirty-eight."

"Is *that* old?"

"Horribly old. Your mother continues to astonish scientists."

While they're occupied, he carefully searches the

backyard, first from the kitchen window, then from the porch. Nothing. He steps into the yard, over leaves he hasn't raked since fall, circles the barbecue pit and the tree, and returns to the house. The kids have fallen asleep.

He awakes to the smell of something burning, runs to the kitchen, and finds Toby holding a stack of mail over the right-front burner of the stove.

"What're you doing," Adams asks.

Toby turns off the stove and tosses the charred envelopes onto the kitchen table. "You didn't open them," he says.

"Get dressed," Adams tells him. "Wake your sister for me."

He drops Toby and Deidre off at their house. "I'm late." He kisses Pamela's cheek—habit—and she steps back. They smile at each other, embarrassed. "Sorry," he says.

On the wall above his desk Carter has a plaque, a quotation from Thomas Jefferson: "No duty the executive had to perform was so trying as to put the right man in the right place."

He introduces Adams to Richard Feldstein, an IBM rep. Feldstein is a short man, thin, with thick black glasses.

"Sam, I've asked Dick to speak to our core group. As you know, we're bringing some hardware in later this month and I want to prepare everyone for the changes."

"Do you have any experience with computer-assisted cartography," Feldstein asks.

"Limited," Adams says.

"Usually we encounter a little resistance at first. People aren't used to computers, they're intimidated, and so on. I want to assure you that your job will be much easier with our equipment."

"We'll allot small amounts of computer time to anyone who wants it," Carter says. "Of course, since you'll be doing special projects for me, you'll have greater access to the software, hmm?"

Adams nods.

"We're providing firm resolution flatbed plotters which will give you approximately 1/25,000 resolution on any surface area," Feldstein explains. "Our power of resolution exceeds data currency at this point, but you'll be prepared when new data becomes available."

"What all this means, Sam, is that you'll be freed from map-making tasks," Carter says. "You'll have time to select the best techniques. Your decisions, stored in the computer, will be more easily defensible. If a map design is flawed, it can be changed at the last minute."

"Our new products include video displays, controls to rotate, distend, or manipulate maps in various manners, as well as synchronized real-time displays," Feldstein says. "The possibilities are astounding. You could provide the medical community with, say, a map of the brain."

"How does it sound, Sam?" Carter asks.

"Terrific. I'm looking forward to it."

"Good. Stop by my office tomorrow morning. I've got a new project for you."

The children have a secret—a whistle deep in their throats. They'll use it against him when he comes to get them, he'll have to be taken away. Of course it's *his* whistle. He gave it to them when he let them have his eyes, nose, chin. It is the whistle his father passed on to him, warning, "Don't blow on it unless you're in terrible trouble. It's a horrible thing that happens when you blow on it. First, a big old hound—he'd be black if you could see him, but no one can see him—leaps on your enemy's neck. Then eleven pairs of white-gloved hands reach out of the air and drag him away by the head. The main thing is, never *never* use it against people you love. Okay?"

And he didn't, but now his children have the whistle and they're angry. He can see it in the way they whisper together, hands on hips. He's come to take them for the evening, away from their mother, the box of broken crayons, the houseful of lost buttons, they don't like it, they don't want to go, not tonight, we want to watch TV, not now, we're warning you. They advance toward him, menacing, he reaches for the door. Too late, they've sounded the alarm. Hot breath on his neck. *Tell us why, tell us why!* the children shout. Eleven pairs of white-gloved hands pin him to the floor.

"Sam," says Carter, "I want you to research twenty-three hundred acres of land in northern Elgin County. The Deerbridge Road area." He offers Adams a Styrofoam cup full of coffee. "Keep this under wraps, but we've got a hell of a real estate deal in the works. I want to know who owns that land and how much they paid for it. Then I'll ask you to draw a map."

He explains in broad terms that On-Line wants to develop northern Elgin County for farm production.

Is it a conflict of interest for a cartographic outfit to buy real estate?

"Use the new hardware. And keep in mind, this is an important project for me personally, hmm?"

In the elevator after work, or in the car, invisible fragrant skin rubs against him, a gift of his thoughts. You are a capable man, he tells himself, deserving of rich rewards. If called upon, you could design a more perfect union, or plan a covert action pleasing to all races (especially the oppressed, who have stowed their pilfered M-16s in four inches of rice-water and mud).

An exquisitely capable man. Everything under one roof: his wife's secret ledger, the children's active sleep. Each morning he woke before dawn. The car wanted in, just to sit with him, he could hear it tapping the back door with its bumper.

But Dad. A silver, room-length pendulum, up and back. But Dad but Dad but Dad.

He reaches for an unshattered glass. Denial was my only promise, kids, didn't I teach you? Stand up straight. Don't flinch, you'll want to kiss each cut. Place your hands on either side, this way, good, stretch it tight until it tears, let the sweetness breathe.

Pamela has a new barbecue pit and paper Chinese lanterns, a No-Pest Strip and wind chimes made of shells. Her lawn is neatly clipped, azaleas beginning to bloom.

Adams, alone with the kids, shuts the sliding glass door against the evening heat. He feels as though he's visiting the home of a distant aunt. The furniture is familiar, but the house itself is strange to him, bright, open, feminine: light colors, cotton doilies, perfumed air.

Pamela, visiting a sick friend, had asked Adams to stop by after work to stay with the kids for a couple of hours. "There's some hamburger in the fridge if you want to barbecue for them," she said.

Now the kids are rolling on the floor, holding their stomachs. The meat seemed fresh, the pickles and lettuce brand-new. Adams himself feels fine. He feeds them aspirin. Deidre can't keep it down. He cups her hot forehead as she leans over the toilet.

"I think that's all."

"Okay, I'll get you a towel."

"No, wait." Another minute, swaying over the bowl.

"Feel better?"

"I think so."

He helps her unbutton her dress. She turns away from him modestly, pulls the dress over her head, and with her back still to him runs to her bed and hides herself under the covers. Adams hangs the dress in the closet full of blocks and books. The puffy sleeves settle, sighing, over the Grinch and the Slippery-Boo. He rubs her stomach through the covers and turns out the light. "Try to sleep," he says.

Toby, meanwhile, has put himself to bed.

"How do you feel?"

"Stopped up."

"Lungs, or just your nose?"

"Just my nose, I guess. And my ears. My throat's sore."

Adams places his hand under Toby's jaw. A slight swelling. He goes into the kitchen and stirs salt into a glass of warm water. "Here, gargle this and spit. Don't swallow."

Neither child can sleep, and by the time Pamela gets home Adams himself feels a little dizzy.

"The hamburger must've been bad," he says.

"Fastway's meat is usually fresh."

The following morning he feels better, but the kids remain in bed for another two days.

He draws a map of no place in particular, circular, many levels like smoke rings. The bottom ring he fills with leaves. Mixed among the leaves, utilizing their stems as definition, twelve brown hawks, wings folded, talons cramped and curled. On the next level the leaves give way to a grid, open squares within which larger hawks are just beginning to unfold their wings and open their eyes. The grid has become so wide on the next level that it can barely be perceived, and the hawks soar beyond the established border, the uneven edges of their feathers defining a new, amorphous territory. Ground to sky, intimacy to infinite space.

Three families own a total of eighteen hundred acres north of Deerbridge Road. Ownership of the remaining five hundred acres is being contested in court. The area looks fertile, grassy, slightly hilly. Streams wind through limestone gullies.

Carter is delighted. "A detailed map, hmm? Analyze movement from the point of view of convenience and cost. Say, within the week. Use the computer."

In Adams' office, a sleek plastic terminal. Keyboard. Blank screen. When he sits in front of the machine his own pale face stares back.

He has two problems: (1) the county line will not be firmly established until the courts act, and (2) he has no starting point.

With a space of uncertain dimensions, where does he begin? In a room, with a piece of furniture—the hutch or the wrought-iron plant stand. But in an undistinguished landscape (i.e., no meteor craters or industrial explosion sites) he is forced to choose at random. If the dimensions of the designated area are in question, the center is arbitrary.

Adams calls the center Point of View. Once this is established, he can arrange all of the territory in sight.

Outside Carter's office, a young secretary crossing and uncrossing her legs. Her desk is aluminum, her typewriter IBM. When Carter is out of the office she pulls a Sony Walkman out of her desk drawer and types to Men at Work or Eddie Money. Partitions made of soundproof tiles separate her from other young secretaries crossing and uncrossing their legs. The partitions stop short of the ceiling; the secretaries do not enjoy complete privacy. Separated just enough so they can't talk to one another.

Carter's secretary smiles at Adams whenever he waits for an appointment. When he speaks to her, he has noticed, she takes her left shoe off underneath the desk. She does not remove this shoe for everyone.

The face of a candidate peeling off a billboard in the rain. Wings of paper whirl to the street, hauling eyebrows, corners of the mouth, the kindly I'll-care-for-you look. A gentle father falling to earth on the backs of furry animals. They come to roost finally in a dark and fertile sewer where the father feels at home. His best tricks are underground tricks: withholding praise from the children, riddling them with anxiety in order to keep them sharp; tempering the wife with a weekly allowance, not mentioning the actual amount in the checking account. He must guard against free-floating pleasure, the anima, the id. He parcels out, in moderation, Dirty Harry movies to the kids, carefully counts the number of Bonwit-Teller boxes his wife brings home. He wallows in the brackish water, pleased with himself.

Overhead, thick copper cables—naked, uninsulated—break through chinks in the stone. Water drips on chalky bricks, splattering the copper. My God, he thinks, examining the wires, the whole city could blow, am I the only one who knows? Fleck fleck, like the ticking of a bomb. He reaches through the tunnels for his kids, no use, he can't find them in time. Sparks burst through manholes, the metal lids go flying, then—

When Deidre was little he held her in his lap and sang

"A bottle of beer turned upside down
Now all the beer is gone"

She laughed and laughed and laughed. Then, one night when she had laughed herself red in the face, she paused, squinched up her nose, and thought about the song. Finally she said, "Daddy, what's the funny of it?"

The children are sick again. Vomiting. Swollen glands. This time, Pamela says, it isn't food poisoning. "We've been eating fresh vegetables."

The doctor finds no traces of infection in either Toby or Deidre. "These look like allergic reactions," he tells Adams, pointing out mild rashes on their arms. "Get some calamine lotion and see if that doesn't clear it up." Pamela takes them to a specialist, but by now the kids are fine, the swelling in their necks has disappeared. The allergy doctor places them each on a table, face down, and with a needle lightly scratches their backs. Next she pours various colored powders on each of the scratches. "These things contain active agents from pollens, spores, cat and dog hair, and so on."

The tests come up negative.

"You've got two healthy kids," the doctor says.

But a week later both are vomiting so hard their stomachs ache. They're crying, awake all night. Pamela is having dizzy spells, too. Adams is convinced they're being poisoned.

"Are you near a toxic waste dump?" He marches in the high grass of the fields around the house in all directions. Old tin cans, shoe soles, carburetor parts.

"I don't think so," Pamela says.

"Then it's in the house. Something in the house is rotten."

The gas stove doesn't leak, the tap water tests fresh. There are no cracks in the foundation, nothing in the attic. "Who lived here before you? A doctor? Were there any old medicine bottles in the trash?"

"No. Nothing. The place was immaculate."

He peels off a strip of wallpaper and examines the wood and chalk underneath. He takes apart one of Deidre's Dr. Seuss books and picks at the dried glue on the binding. Everything in the garage he throws out, even clean white rags and unopened cans of motor oil.

Deidre has lost six pounds.

He takes Toby and Deidre back to the allergy specialist. "Something is killing my children."

She runs another series of tests over the next two weeks. Nothing turns up.

He sits on his bed with a brandy. Evening, changing light. Each minute another noise stilled: birds, cars, plastic pails. Dinner's over, up and down the street. Same old meats. No one's going out. His mind turns round.

The glass falls off the night table. Getting up he knocks his foot against the bed. "Goddammit!" he yells. He'll raze the backyard fence, torch the weeds, drive through the plate-glass window at the downtown office of H&R Block. He'll commandeer the local CBS affiliate and broadcast nasty rumors about the East Coast, the NRA, the national debt—a lovely day in the neighborhood. Top with pineapple sauce, bake for three hours. Right back, we'll be right back. One two three four, try it at home now. His rage a clear white river through town.

Adams notices that the grass around Pamela's barbecue pit is dying. He picks and sniffs a handful of yellow blades. The barbecue pit is rusty—it's brand-new!—and discolored. With his handkerchief Adams clears away the charcoal. The metal at the bottom of the pit is mottled yellow and green. Heat wouldn't have done that. He asks Pamela where she purchased the barbecue pit.

"At a wholesaler's. A big discount warehouse north of town," she says.

"Take me there."

Hundreds of cars are parked in the fields around the warehouse, and families of shoppers are walking through rows of plastic birdbaths, lawn statuary, clay pots, wind chimes, garden tools. Inside, fishing corks, tire irons, bicycle speedometers, Coleman lanterns, decks of cards. The barbecue pits, identical with Pamela's, occupy a corner. The first two salesmen Adams encounters know nothing about them except how much they cost. The third salesman says they're made from metal drums.

"Where'd you get the metal drums?"

He doesn't know. Adams presses. The salesman guides him to the warehouse manager.

"We bought them in bulk from a little outfit called Drum Corps."

"What was in them before you bought them?"

"I don't know. What's the problem?"

"I suspect your barbecue pit is poisoning my children."

The man laughs, then sees that Adams is serious. "Honestly, I don't know. They're a little outfit that collects drums from various companies, cleans them up, and sells them to wholesalers like us for storage or, in our case, barbecue pits."

Adams insists on locating Drum Corps. The manager tries to talk him out of it, but relents when Adams mentions the Better Business Bureau.

Drum Corps is located seventy-five miles east of Elgin. Adams cannot find a telephone number, so the following Saturday he drives to the address given him by the manager. Meanwhile, he has told Pamela not to use the barbecue pit, and to keep the kids away from it.

An old Sinclair gas station, the dinosaur still on its sign, has become the Drum Corps office. Where the gas pumps were, tortured metal strips twist out of the concrete holding a square of splintered wood, about the size of a car door, with DRUM CORPS painted on it. Rusty barrels and drums, half eaten, badly stained. A grizzled collie sleeps near a stack of metal lids.

Adams parks his car by the side of the road. Old cotton fields, fallow now, stretch for miles behind the station. The sun is clear but cold. A young man in a Pink Floyd T-shirt and dusty desert boots walks out of the station, drinking a bottled Coke. "Help you?"

"Yeah. Are you the people who sold a bunch of drums to the wholesale warehouse in Elgin?"

"Might be. Have to check. My dad's the one who runs things but he's out fishing."

"Could you check for me?"

"Sure."

They go inside. An Italian auto parts calendar featuring a naked brunette and a shock absorber curls on the wall. The calendar is open to October 1973.

"Yeah, 'bout six months ago. Why?"

"Can you tell me what was in those drums?"

The boy laughs. "No way of knowing. We get 'em from all over. California, Texas, Louisiana."

"Who do you get them from?"

"Chemical plants, oil refineries . . . you'd have to ask my dad." He makes a loud sucking noise with the bottle.

"What's your name?"

"Bo."

"Bo, does your dad know these things are dangerous?"

"No, man, we steam-clean 'em before we sell 'em. Twice. Everything is steam-cleaned twice, kills everything, all the germs and everything."

"I've got a couple of kids at home who've been sick for two months—ever since my wife brought home a barbecue pit made with one of these things."

"Hey, we don't *make* anything. We just sell 'em."

Adams glances out the dirty window. In the pale sunlight, the sight of the rusty orange drums, with their thin eaten edges, tiny holes like cavities in a child's teeth, and tarnished yellow rings, makes the back of his neck prickle.

"When will your dad be back?"

"Not till tomorrow."

Adams nods. A dust devil swirls along the edge of the highway, ripping light weeds from the ground. The collie looks up. "Okay, thanks."

"Hey, look, we make sure the things are clean. Maybe your kids have colds or something."

"I'll be back," Adams says.

One night several months before their separation, Pamela read to him in bed excerpts from Paul Klee's diary. " 'I am abstract with memories. . . . What takes place is merely an approximation.' "

"I admire his orderly mind," Pamela said. "I aspire to it. He numbered every thought.

" 'Many variations on the theme Father and Son. A father with his son. A father through his son. A father in the presence of his son. A father proud of his son. A father blesses his son.' "

The following morning, Adams scribbled on a sheet of tracing paper:

1) Father removes half-inch pc. yellow chalk from son's right nostril.

2) Father ignores wet diaper until son pours oatmeal on radio.

3) Father teaches son to shoot BB rifle, to consternation of neighbor's knee.

The Better Business Bureau confirms that steam-cleaning cannot effectively neutralize all chemical compounds. Drum Corps has been receiving drums from shipyards in the Texas gulf and from a drilling company in Southern California. In addition, medical centers and utility companies have sent them barrels, some of which contain low-level radioactive waste. Traces of benzene, toluene, and sulfuric acid have been found in the "clean" barrels. Seven months ago the bureau issued a warning to Drum Corps. Adams' efforts have closed them for good. The wholesale warehouse has been fined two thousand dollars.

Deidre sprawls on the floor reading the adventures of Curious George and Babar, King of the Elephants. Toby wheezes, finishing his homework.

Pamela stands with Adams over the dead spot in the backyard.

"I've had nightmares," she says. "The kids' bones all twisted."

The doctors have decided there will be no permanent effects from the exposure, but Adams has dreamed disaster, too: Deidre's ovaries knotted like thick hard rope, Toby's lungs exploded like paper sacks. He thinks of their first child, Alan, swimming among molecules as large as billiard balls. He remembers a plastic model of DNA in a college laboratory, the double helix that resembled an unfinished staircase into the hallway of infinity. But he can't keep his mind on infinity, or Alan, this morning. Babar, King of the Elephants, glows in the dark. Yertle the Turtle, with red unseeing eyes, lights the floor of the sea.

Part Two

I WANT them back.

He wakes with this sentence. He had dreamed of his grandparents, all of whom are dead now. In the dream they were walking, the four of them together, on a rope-and-wooden bridge over a stream in a park heavy with foliage. White feathers rained from the trees and the grandparents were laughing, sharing a bottle of wine with napkins and plastic cups. Adams watched them from a distance, seated at a red cedar table, thinking how much the grandparents could've taught him about history, marriage, politics. But when they were alive, he was a small child, not yet ready for their lessons, and he knew in the dream that he couldn't go to them. He began to regret that for much of his life his timing has been off with people who might've proved important. Relations, friends, possible lovers. People he relinquished when circumstances made friendship too difficult.

I'm not done with them. I want them back. Toby and Deidre too.

The unfinished business with his children sends him to the kitchen. There's only a little apple juice left in the refrigerator, so he pours a cup and stands at the window to toast his family, here and gone.

Pamela's hair color remains the same (rich auburn), she has gained no weight (one hundred and ten pounds, consistently, since college), but her attitudes are shading into gray, she's reading more books, and her thoughts are changing her, physically, from the inside out. She looks younger than Adams and talks like someone he has never met. On Saturday she attended a pro-Palestinian rally; she plans to march in protest of American military presence in Honduras.

"Where are your politics these days?" he asks.

"On the left, where my heart is."

Already he has spent hundreds of dollars on Pamela's work, and now she's asked him for a loan. At forty-one thousand a year, with a family of four, he is nearly underwater.

He sits in front of the TV with a bag of Doritos and a pocket calculator. Frank Gifford informs him that Tom Landry is the only coach the Dallas Cowboys have ever had.

In the last three years his social security tax has risen from $2,346 a year to $3,407. Even with the latest tax cut he figures to absorb a net loss this year of over six hundred dollars and will have to spend part of his savings.

The kids' bills will be about the same—higher dental costs, perhaps—but Pamela is unpredictable. And he never knows when Kenny will have an emergency, like the time he was arrested in Buster Keaton's old house with three actresses and a bag of coke. One of the women, subletting the house from its current owners, took the rap—"I don't touch the stuff," Kenny said—but the incident cost Adams five hundred dollars for bail.

Before she left, Pamela developed a series of holograms based on the work of Dieter Jung, a German photographer and painter. She had attended an exhibition of Jung's "Spanned Rainbows," depictions of light in oil. The word *Wirklichkeit* occurred to her as she viewed the paintings. "*Wirklichkeit* means everything we know," she explained to Adams. "It's inseparable from *Werk*, to work, and *wirken*, to effect."

Pamela cherishes her German ancestry (her father's mother came from Siegen) and, to Adams, her pride recalls their days at the University of Nebraska. Pamela had been a commercial photographer, active in local publishing though only a sophomore, and Adams had distinguished himself as an outstanding student in the geology department. As his graduate studies progressed, he became increasingly interested in contour charts and even secured a number of grants for surveys. At night, in the lobby of her dorm, Pamela discussed her plans with Adams. "Photography's an art, but I can't afford to be fancy. I've got to earn some money."

After graduation Adams went to Alaska for two months on a postdoctoral grant from Conoco, leaving Pamela to finish school. That summer she did free-lance work (the AP picked up her shot of lightning striking the state capitol in Lincoln) and took a night course in the history of photography. In August she had a gallery showing with two friends. She had made a series of double exposures—celery super-imposed on a farm laborers' rally—and tinted them, each a different color. Though the response was good, she didn't take it seriously and concentrated on journalism. Then she got chummy with a few fashion designers for whom she did Sunday-supplement ads.

The day she returned from the Jung exhibit she leaped and sang. Her eyes narrowed, thin as almonds, and she played with the ends of her hair. "If you make the viewer aware of the *materials* of art—the pigment in the paint, the emulsion on the film," she said, "you've performed a critical as well as an artistic act. It's what I've been looking for in my work."

Suddenly fashion ads were out. At dinner she lectured him on aesthetics. A grid can be centrifugal or centripetal. When Mondrian paints a vertical and horizontal grid and places it within a diamond-shaped canvas, cutting off the corners of the grid, our view is truncated but we know that the painter's landscape continues beyond what we can see. On the other hand, grid lines can act as a divider between the world of the canvas and the space that the viewer occupies. The prevalence of the grid in modern art, and its profound ambiguity, reveal the depths to which our century is divided between the sacred and the secular, the inner and outer worlds. The grid is essentially materialistic, of course, despite what Malevich says about Mind and Spirit or the Greek cross in Ad Reinhardt's nine-square grids.

Adams didn't know what she was talking about.

She traced the roots of *Wirklichkeit*. Originally, she discovered, *Werk* and *wirken* meant to wrap with wicker. To medieval Germans, the empirical world was woven from a variety of materials, including earth, air, water, and fire. Each man or woman was a knot or straw.

Next, Pamela tested the limits of her equipment. With nails she scratched patterns on her negatives. On long exposures she alternated light and dark, oscillated color, and formed swirls—like fingerprints or cloth swatches—with different intensities of light.

Within a month she had borrowed holographic equipment from her friend Cyndi. "A hologram looks three-dimensional, but it's not. It's formed by curved space and pulsating light," she explained. "A map of our cognition."

Her first images were conventional: butterflies, cats, sparkling rocks, each structured like a feather. One chilly night in February, sleet pelting the windows,

Pamela called Adams into the garage. "Look," she said, switching off the light.

In the air, twisting above the vise grip, the word *Wirklichkeit*. Aquamarine. Wrapped in wicker. Rippling like a wave, or Adams' breath.

She was making progress. It made him uneasy.

Adams asks Carter's secretary, whose name is Jill, to dinner. She accepts. He makes reservations for two at the Ivory Rose, which has the best Indian food in town. It turns out that Jill is, like Adams, a world traveler. Over curry and chutney she tells him she once had an Algerian lover. In Algeria there were no working toilets. She had to squat over an open hole, wipe herself with her left hand.

Since returning from Algeria she has attended a number of *est* seminars. "I was raised a Baptist, but their ideas about women are skewed. I mean, be submissive and all that. Don't have sex. Shit. Who are they kidding? The Gospel writers—excuse me, this isn't good dinner conversation, I know—but they didn't have to walk around with tampons between their legs, know what I mean? The preachers don't know what it's like. So I figure, whatever the church says about women's bodies and sexual behavior and all that, they don't know the first thing. Those decisions I make for myself. *est* is hokey in a lot of ways, but they let you make up your own mind, and you can walk away anytime you like." She sugars her tea. "A lot of people are turned off by *est*."

"I don't know much about it."

"Be honest. What did you think when I brought it up?"

"I wondered if you were—"

"A fruitcake, right? Be honest."

"Yes," Adams says. "I did."

"That's okay. *est* has that reputation, but it's an easy target, you see. Anything really personal is easy to laugh at, don't you think?"

"Sure, because nobody knows what it is."

"Exactly." She looks away, suddenly shy. "I'm sorry, Sam, I probably *am* coming on like a fruitcake. It's been a long week, you know? I haven't had a chance to unwind."

"It's okay. I'm enjoying it."

"Me, too." She smiles. "I just don't want you to think I'm one of those dizzy secretaries or anything. Actually, I think *est* is pretty stupid. It gave me something to do when I first got back to the States. What really interests me is the stock market. I watched it for a year, then started investing. Made thirty-two hundred bucks the first five months."

"You're kidding."

"You got to watch these high-tech industries. They're springing up everywhere and if you hit the right one you're off and sailing, but lots of them go bust right away. I wish I'd been old enough to get in on air conditioning in the early days. That's the place to be. What about you?" she says. "What are your values in life?"

The question is troublesome, but not without charm. "I like my work," he says.

"Yeah, but Carter's a smoothie, isn't he? I could see him in the Nixon administration or something. He'll make a lot of money for the company, but I wouldn't vouch for his ways and means."

"I'm glad I'm not the only one who feels that way."

At home, Adams offers her Drambuie. For the first time he looks carefully at her body. He'd found her attractive at work, but any slender woman with blond hair who is the boss's secretary achieves a kind of status. He senses that, in sexual matters, she is not a patient woman.

Her left shoe has come off. Discreetly, Adams nudges the shoe away from her foot. "Would you like to go to bed?"

"Yes, I think so." She places her glass on the coffee table. "We should make a process note first."

"A what?"

"It's kind of silly, but sometimes you learn something. We should admit to each other, honestly, how this evening affected us."

"All right."

"How do you feel," she asks.

"Fine."

"Can you elaborate?"

"I'd like to make love to you."

She wants to know why. Adams doesn't say anything. She accepts that.

. . .

Chopping vegetables for the children's dinner, Adams listens tight-lipped to Toby complain about congestion in his chest.

"Mom gets me these pills."

"What kind of pills?"

"Oxydol, I think."

"That's a detergent, Toby. What about an antihistamine?"

"They don't work."

His seditious illness. When he was smaller, rather than do what Adams said, he gasped like a sun-bleached fish. *I was born wrong*, his face seemed to say. "I'll dream for you a day of air," Adams promised. "Leaping, running, baseballs falling slowly in the blue, blue sky." But at night his lungs glowed blue with exertion through the sheets. This was Toby's way of fighting him. Adams thought of Alan, pink fists flailing in the air, waving good-bye.

Deidre's body is as strong as a missile. Setting the table, she stretches as if health were as easy to hold as a fork. But Adams anticipates failure. He pictures Deidre a few years older, chipping away at her body piece by piece with PCP and pot, group sex and artificial coloring agents. Driving her home from dance class one evening in late winter, he passed a young boy walking barefoot in the snow, shirt unbuttoned, mouth open to the cold and sleet. Deidre pointed, frightened. "What's wrong with him, Dad?" Adams pulled up beside him, rolling down his window. "Are you all right?" he said. "Can we help you?" The boy didn't even know they were there. He plowed through drifts of snow, flapping his arms in the headlights.

"Is he crazy?" Deidre said.

"I think he's taken some kind of drug."

They followed him slowly for half a block, then three squad cars surrounded him in the middle of the street, spotlighting him with their flashing lights. He put his arms over his eyes and began to scream; four policemen were needed to subdue him. Deidre started to cry. For a long time after that she refused to take even aspirin, and is still wary of medicines, but Adams, exercising his fatherly right, imagines the worst for her teenage years.

Isohyet, from the Greek: *isos*, equal; *hyetos*, rain. A line drawn on a map to indicate equal rainfall along its length.

Twice a year the employees of On-Line Information Systems are required to see the company psychologist, a muttering, bent man named Mayer. He does not submit anyone to rigorous testing, merely asks questions related to work. A week later he types a psychological profile of each employee, listing his/her managerial strengths, social limitations, etc. In rare cases he recommends that someone attend a personal growth seminar, tax-deductible.

Adams is scheduled for Monday morning at eleven.

At 10:55 he sits waiting in the foyer. Jordan bolts from Dr. Mayer's office.

"What's the matter with him," Adams asks.

"Nothing, nothing," the doctor says.

"Bad day?"

"He's under a bit of a strain right now. As who isn't?" Mayer says.

"I've been worried about him for a long time."

"Oh?"

"Yeah. He seems a little weird to me."

"You all know I'm here. If he's having problems, he knows where to come."

Adams nods. "Maybe I shouldn't tell you this, but I think he's been standing in my yard."

"Really?"

"Well, not lately. But I'm sure it was him. And there's nothing to see, I mean, I don't know what he was looking for. It gave me the creeps. I called the police but they wouldn't do anything."

"Have you spoken to him about it?"

"He denies it." Jordan, in fact, had merely laughed in his typical offhand manner.

"Let me know if you see him again."

The doctor asks Adams a series of questions, such as, "When you are under deadline pressure and fear you won't make it, do you (a) give up, (b) request an extension, (c) work harder to finish, (d) other."

The following Monday, Adams receives his profile in the interoffice mail: "A conscientious worker and careful listener. A tendency toward abstraction, even in the most casual conversations. Best production when allowed to proceed at his own pace, though he responds well to pressure. Uncomfortable in groups, prefers to work alone."

He's had friends. Fathers like himself who've sacrificed exciting careers as anglers, goalies, and entrepreneurs to raise their children. Watching baseball on Saturday afternoon with one such friend, he encountered, face-to-face, the sadness that grips certain fathers. "Right there. That was me. I was up for that part," his friend said. On the screen a man putted around a toilet bowl in a boat. "Katie was pregnant. Insisted there wasn't enough security in acting, so I went to work for State Farm." His friend gazed wistfully at the little boat. "Ah well, what the hell," he said. "I insure suckers ten times that size."

Potency is an ugly thing.

Still, thinking back, fathering was perhaps *the* source of erotic mystery for Adams—a sleeplessness beneath his pleasure with Pamela at night.

There was a park by the house where they lived in the days before Deidre was born. Adams walked there with Toby. In the evenings other fathers joined him. Softballs, footballs. The clink of skate keys against nickels and dimes, money for ice cream, in the fathers' heavy pockets. He remembers a group of young women and men marching up the street past the park, carrying signs. It was the early seventies. The last legs of the youth movement, they were denouncing Richard Nixon with not much conviction. Their signs read STOP THE BOMBING IN CAMBODIA and ANDY WARHOL FOR PRESIDENT.

"Daddy, who's Andy Warhol," asked a neighbor's daughter.

"No one knows, honey," her father said.

Now that neighbor's in Seattle—like other fathers, he hit the road in service of free enterprise. Hundreds of fathers balancing themselves on the white stripes of the highways, wives and children stacked on their shoulders as high as ice cream cones.

Other fathers have died. Adams misses them. He shared many terrifying moments with them, signing release forms in emergency rooms, squirming in metal folding chairs in recital halls. They taught the little girls how to blow their noses without bursting their eardrums, and the little boys how to scratch their balls, if scratch they must, in secret, through their pockets. They were good fathers, all of them, full of love for their wives and gratitude for a cold glass of beer, with failing legs but the courage to dive for any wild pitch that came their way.

He finds an excuse to visit the Records Office. As he's thumbing through the photo file, he asks Jordan, "Everything all right?"

"Yeah."

"I think those visits with Mayer are a waste of time, don't you? He says the same thing every time."

"He's all right," Jordan says. "He isn't a gung-ho company man like everybody else around here. It's refreshing."

Adams wonders if he has just been insulted. "Has he ever said anything you could use?"

"What business is that of yours?"

"Nothing. Wasn't personal. I just don't find his little profiles very helpful."

Jordan puts down the stack of 8 x 10's he's been holding. "I don't know what this thing is that you seem to have about me, Sam, but I wish you'd stop it. I've never seen your fucking yard, all right? And I'll tell you something else, if I need to see Mayer, it's because *you're* driving me crazy."

He pours himself a beer and opens a bag of chips. He walks to the living room, sits at his drafting table, studies his latest map of the property Carter has recently acquired.

Something is wrong. What is it?

The isohyet. What about it?

The ninety-eighth meridian.

Adams squints, sips his beer.

When someone fouls up, the volume of mail passing back and forth within On-Line increases dramatically. Interoffice memos travel between floors, beginning "Earlier we discussed . . ." or "In reference to last week's conference . . ." Each department goes on record as having been clean.

The company library, containing a number of atlases and journals, is located in a niche off the coffee room. There, on a shelf along one wall, a row of legal books entitled *Words and Phrases* can be found. These volumes provide legal definitions for every occasion. When a problem arises within the company, the books disappear from the library.

Carter's got his lawyers, Mallow and Vox, working overtime on the real estate deals. Vox is a tiny man, lost in his clothes. His face is as battered as a drum head, ravaged, it appears, from serious bouts with acne. Adams has never had a direct conversation with him, talks past him in meetings.

Mallow is nervous and pale. Adams hasn't had occasion to work with him, either, but knows from the newsletter that he has lobbied in Washington with lawyers from corporations in their congressional district. In addition, both Mallow and Vox have formed, at Carter's request, a Political Action Committee. Company policy states that management-level personnel must contribute to the committee. The rest of the employees are not required to do so, but know that failure to give is interpreted by Carter as refusal to support the company's goals.

When Mallow comes around, pale hand hanging open, Adams makes a point of giving a little more each time.

. . .

The offending left hand: On the freeway Adams waves to the world. He signals waiters and cashiers with his left hand. With his left hand he acknowledges Jordan from across the coffee room. When he speaks to Pamela on the phone, he holds the receiver in his left hand.

"The other night Deidre woke me up and said a bad clown had come out of her coloring book and tried to stick his puffy cap down her throat," Pamela says. "She couldn't understand why I didn't search her room. Then I thought, if she can't tell the difference between waking life and dreams, and if there's anything at all to Aristotle's notion that the pleasure of art is imitation, then Deidre can't appreciate art. She doesn't *know* it's imitation. So I bought a clown suit—"

"Pam?" Adams says. "Are you terrorizing our daughter?"

Pamela laughs. "It's true. There was no pleasure on her face."

Mosquitoes swarm around his arms. He passes the Polish dance hall and the cemetery that round off one end of his neighborhood (it has never been zoned). Rosa the fortune-teller is standing on her front porch in a print dress, a purple scarf draped around her head. She picks her teeth with a toothpick, gazes at the tombstones across the street.

In the public library, two blocks from his house,

Adams finds books on climatology, geography, and federal land grant programs. He carries the books to a wooden table and switches on the green reading lamp.

The ninety-eighth meridian. Of course.

At the turn of the century, American meteorologists drew a thirty-inch isohyet along the ninety-eighth meridian, indicating the westernmost boundary along which the annual rainfall averaged thirty inches. Thirty inches, along with rate of evaporation and seasonal distribution, was, according to the meteorologists, the bare minimum needed to grow crops. Carter's property lies west of the line.

"You're making an awful lot of noise about a thirty-inch line," Carter says.

"That line could be very important to a number of families."

"The county averages over forty inches of rain a year."

"Yes, but the rainfall isn't evenly distributed. In the fall, parts of the county experience droughtlike conditions. The land looks fertile, but those are limestone hills containing only surface soil. Those shrubs are stunted trees."

"Granted, it won't be easy to cultivate. . . ."

"It'll be impossible to cultivate."

"Damn it, Sam, you're too smart for your own good," Carter says, leaning forward in his chair.

"I suggest—"

"How do you like your computer?"

"I like it very much."

"We've got to pay for it, hmm?"

"Yes."

"Hmm?"

"Sure."

"Then move the isohyet a quarter of an inch to the left," Carter says.

"Excuse me?"

"After all, the county records aren't all that accurate." Carter opens the office door. "And while you're at it, draw up a mental map of the area and an environmental stress chart of the county."

A foul-up: City council, at the request of its senior member, a former Spenserian scholar, renames one of its residential streets Faerie Queene Boulevard. Tenants in apartments on Faerie Queene Boulevard move out. Owners complain that they cannot rent property in the area.

Several thousand maps have been printed, bearing the name Faerie Queene Boulevard.

Memos fly back and forth—first within city hall, then between city hall and On-Line, finally within On-Line itself. Thousands of tax dollars later, *Words and Phrases* reappears on the shelves of the company library.

A recipe comes in the mail. Stew with steak. He makes it for Jill.

"Scrumptious," she says, scooting next to him on the bed. "Your recipe?"

"The power company's. It came with their bill."

"Bless them," Jill says.

He pulls her to his chest. She asks about his wife. "She works at the high school," he tells her, "balancing PA speakers in the rafters of the boys' gymnasium."

"Tell me about your kids."

"I've hired them out to the fair. They have to push the Ferris wheel all day long to keep it spinning."

She laughs. He looks past her through the window. Outside her apartment on a billboard, a whiskey ad: a giant glass, ice tumbling over blocks of ice.

Toby has flunked his science class—inevitable, like the failure of the city's fiscal plan and the raising of taxes, but disheartening nevertheless. Toby does not seem upset at the prospect of summer school.

"What does your mother say about it?" Adams says.

"She wants to send me to a doctor."

"What kind of doctor?"

"A shrink."

"We'll see about that."

"Is there any peach ice cream," Deidre asks.

"Yes, but finish your hot dog first."

After dinner Adams walks with them past the Polish dance hall and the cemetery. The evening is cool.

The kids enjoy poking around the old neighborhood. Deidre still seems to think she'll be back here any day.

They encounter the Reverend Sister Rosa on the sidewalk in front of her house. Toby assumes a defensive stance, Deidre hides behind Adams.

"Why, hello, I haven't seen you in a long time," Rosa says, extending her arm toward Toby.

"Hi," Toby says, stiffly shaking the woman's hand.

"And how are *you*?" Rosa asks, peering around Adams' legs.

"Fine," Deidre answers.

"Lovely evening."

"Yes," says Adams, edging the kids past her.

"I was just getting ready to sit out here on the porch with a plate of spaghetti. Would you like to join me? I made a big pot. You know how it is with spaghetti."

"Thanks, we've eaten."

"I see. Taking a little stroll, then?"

"That's right."

"It's a wonderful neighborhood if you can afford to stay. My husband died six years ago, and it's been a real struggle." She has managed to pay off the house, though, and guesses she'll die in it. "When I'm gone, they won't have far to carry me," she says, nodding at the cemetery across the street.

"We live here, too," Deidre says.

"Used to," Toby corrects her.

"I know what," Rosa says, looking sadly at the

children. "I'll bet the kids would like to have their fortunes told, am I right?"

"We've got to—"

"On me." She winks at Adams. "It'll only take a second and it'll be fun for them. Maybe they'll get lucky in love." Before he can think of a reply, she's headed up her walk, motioning for him to follow.

"Did you know she's a witch?" Deidre whispers, tugging on Adams' pants.

"Shhh," Adams says. "Be friendly."

Rosa's front room is small, lighted by a single lamp with a yellow shade. On the television, underneath the rabbit ears, a stack of newspapers and magazines. Paintings of Jesus and photographs of Eugene Debs cover the walls, garlic stalks wilt in blue vases around the room.

"Can I get you a glass of water?"

The kids shake their heads.

Rosa produces a deck of Tarot cards from her dress pocket and flips through them like a picture book.

"You're first," she tells Toby. "Shuffle the cards, and think about what you'd like to know."

The cards fascinate Adams. He doesn't believe in their ability to foretell the future, but as a symbol system they intrigue him, and he's taken with the idea of mapping time. Instinctively, he reaches for the Two of Wands. It depicts a young man looking over battlements to the sea. In his right hand he grips a small globe; in his left he clutches a staff.

Rosa tells him, "This is the lord of the manor. The card indicates riches, magnificence, dominance, skill in science."

Adams smiles. Rosa adds, "When the card appears upside down in a reading, it indicates sadness, suffering, lack of will."

Adams lays the card aside.

The Nine of Wands—a young man, head wrapped in bandages, leaning on a staff—reminds him of Jordan: the vacant stare, the air of patience and immobility.

"Cunning, hidden strength, opposition," Rosa says, tapping the card. "This person is an able adversary."

The Two of Swords: a blindfolded woman balancing a pair of swords on her shoulders. She sits on a bench with her back to the sea, a crescent moon above. "This would be a very desirable card for you in a reading," Rosa tells him. "It indicates balanced forces, an end to family quarrels. It can also, in rare cases, mean impotence."

Toby will be a great man, Rosa predicts, like Churchill or Kennedy. Deidre will have many children.

"I want to be a great man, too," she says.

"You will, of course you will," Rosa tells her.

The spaghetti is about to boil over on Rosa's stove, and Adams uses this as an excuse to get away. Politely, and with thanks, he hustles the children out the door.

"Listen, I'm starting a group séance on Thursday nights. Ten percent discount if you contact two or more spirits. Drop by sometime."

"Thanks, I will," Adams says.

"She's a neat lady," Deidre muses on the way home. "I liked it, what she said about me."

"I thought you said she was a witch."

"That was before I was a great man."

Adams places his watch on the back porch, next to the barbecue pit. Jordan does not appear. The following evening Adams leaves a ring.

Putting someone in his place
I can't see my way clear
Getting to the bottom of things
That's beneath me
On the straight and narrow
Get lost
Leading someone up the garden path
This is really nowhere

Straightening his desk at the end of the day, he discovers in a stack of papers the program notes from last year's conference on plate tectonics. Over drinks in a hotel lobby a seismologist from UCLA had turned to him. "In an information-based society, what happens to blue-collar workers?" he said. "You and me, information-gatherers, we're the elite. But we're not making plans for people who work with their hands." Adams was tired. He shared a room with Carter, though their schedules overlapped and they didn't see each other much. Carter's presentation had been given a prime spot on the bill—Friday evening, closing night. Adams was relegated to Tuesday afternoon, when many of the conferees were playing tennis or enjoying late lunches.

He ordered another gin and tonic, nodded perfunctorily at his colleague, and tried to spin the ashtray. It was glued to the table. "It's the same lack of foresight that gets us into wars," the seismologist continued. "In a million years the continents will have cracked so much you won't be able to tell America from Spain. We fight and sign treaties as if nothing's going to change, but in a geologically active world, what does territoriality mean?"

"Here's the information you wanted."

"Good, good, come in," says Carter. "What did you find?"

"The Deerbridge Road area is generally perceived as undesirable."

"We've got an ad campaign that'll change that."

"Also, I drew an Ignorance Surface Map. People tend to confuse similar shapes when they're side by side—Arizona and New Mexico are often mistaken for one another. And it occurred to me that Richmond County, which is nothing but scrub oaks, is shaped a little like the northern half of Elgin County. Perhaps people confuse the two, and think your lots are barren."

"Wonderful. We can use that."

"Of course, rainfall amounts being what they are—"

"Right. And the isohyet?"

"Where you wanted it."

"Very good. Do you know what we're doing, Sam? We're educating people's desires."

"You mean, telling them what they want?"

"That's a little hard. Let's say we're paving the way for change. Sit tight, hmm? Phase Two in a couple of days."

Adams tells Carter he will not alter any more maps. Falsifying documents is not what he had in mind when he came to work for On-Line. Besides, prestige does not accompany local projects; overseas fieldwork is the best means of gaining promotion and respect.

"I was hoping for another international assignment," he says. "Now's a particularly good time for me to travel."

"Why's that?"

"My wife and I separated."

"Sorry to hear it."

"Thank you. Anyway, with the kids gone, I have less responsibility at home. I'm a good man in the field, and it's been over two years."

"Your skills are needed here, Sam." He taps the *Ixodes* on Adams' lapel. "At least for the time being.

We'll consider an international assignment in a few months, okay?"

Late at night in his office, Adams fiddles with the console. A single fluorescent bulb buzzes overhead. Below, the street is quiet.

He calls two light cones up on the screen—a pair of pale blue pyramids, points touching in the center of the graph.

The upper light cone he labels *accessible future*: that is, the realm of events that can possibly follow the present. The bottom cone's the *accessible past*: the realm of events leading up to now. The white space outside the light cones is the inaccessible future and past. He has, in effect, drawn the basis of a map defining the regions of the universe knowable from a given point in space and time.

To make the map more accurate, he must concentrate the surface area of the light cones. When he does so, the shape of the cones fluctuates wildly, indicating that the line between future and past can easily blur, even at short distances.

Next, he calls to the screen a wormhole. On a flat plane, a wormhole is formed by drawing two openings opposite each other and stretching them into a single tube. If, as some astronomers believe, dead suns form wormholes in space, the topology around them is highly unstable.

Further, Adams discovers that if he quantizes all the data on the screen, emptiness acquires a complex topology. It looks like an arterial system, a tightly fused matrix of tubes. To fully understand the shape of space-time, he needs a four-dimensional image.

He switches off the system, gets up, stretches, and walks to the window. Tattered paper flutters in the street, against the curb. A couple strolls down the walk. Tiny caterpillars of motion inhabit the space between him and the street where, tomorrow morning at eight, he will enter the building.

In Ecuador, where Adams once headed an international group, the Quechua Indians, an educated and happy people, believe the future lies behind them. "A man does not have eyes in the back of his head," said one. "Nor can he see the future. Does it not make sense, then, to place the future behind you?" Similarly, the past, an "open book," lies ahead.

Adams feels like a Quechua.

At work his supply of ink is low. He hasn't been to the storeroom. Grease pencils aren't precise and lead pencils aren't dark enough. He'll try it anyway.

1:00 He can't see the grids he has made. The lines are simply too light, and his eyes begin to ache. He should have used the computer.

2:00 Deerbridge Road.

2:15 Deerbridge Road disappears. County records are uncertain.

4:45 Deerbridge Road reappears.

At home, he tries to call the kids. No answer.

At dusk, Jordan returns. He is standing close to the house and appears to be fiddling with the faucet. For the first time, Adams feels panic more than curiosity or annoyance. Still in his suit he leaps out the door, past the barbecue pit and the tree. The man turns, opens the gate, flies up the walk. Adams, in pursuit, loosens his tie. The man jumps a fence. Adams follows. Shrubs. Thorns. The barking of a dog. Pale blue television light flickers through blinds. The laughter of the neighbors. Loose bricks in the yards. Dog shit, the smell of lilac. Adams can't keep up—Jordan is much younger than he, and in better shape. "Goddamn you!" Adams calls. The man heaves a plastic garbage can at him. Adams brushes potato skins from his suit, runs up the empty street past the dance hall and Rosa's house. His shoes hurt. The man has disappeared. Did he have a car waiting?

Adams sits on the curb. The night is humid, tar shines on the streets. He can turn left, make a right, or go straight. He can walk backwards up the street until he reaches a dead end.

An airplane passes overhead.

He's not sure where he is.

He clambers over a wire mesh fence and finds himself in a garden. Peppers, tomatoes, beets. A pigeon coop.

As Adams speaks, Mayer remains impassive, remote.

"And you've positively identified him?"

"Well, I think so. It looked like he was doing something to the house. You've treated the man. You must know he's nuts."

Mayer shows him nothing.

"I want to know the best course of action. I've already called the police. I could try them again, or maybe it would be better if you did it. I need a rational plan; otherwise I'm going to fly off the handle. Enough is enough."

"It wouldn't hurt for you to call the police again, ask them to patrol the neighborhood if they will. In the meantime, I'll speak to Mr. Jordan and we'll determine what needs to be done."

"He *is* nuts, right? He sure looked like it the day he came running out of your office."

Mayer says only, "I'll speak to him. There's been no damage to your property, is that correct?"

"Not that I can tell."

"All right, Mr. Adams. Thank you for bringing this to my attention. I know how upsetting something like this can be. If you're having trouble sleeping—"

Mayer follows him into the hall. Jordan is walking toward them from the far end. Adams starts, but Mayer holds his arm. "Please, Mr. Adams, let me speak to him before you say anything, all right?"

Adams straightens his coat. "You asshole," he says to Jordan.

. . .

Inevitably, the call from Pamela's family. He's surprised it didn't come sooner: perhaps they were hoping for a reconciliation by now. Her father, Jurgen, accuses Adams of neglecting Pamela's needs. Without irony, Adams asks, "What *are* her needs?" It seems to him that her needs were ill-defined even at the time of their wedding. Would she be a journalist or an artist? Would she travel with Adams or remain at home? Perhaps she married him because, given her family background, marriage was prudent for her; yet Adams, with his passport and maps, was the most impractical of husbands.

When they met she was taking an Old English course. "Your eyes are Nordic," she said, *winter-ċearig*," which, roughly translated, meant "winter-sad." The fact that she found him moody pleased him at the time. He enjoyed being a serious young student.

Jurgen wanted to marry them but Adams refused politely, feeling that to grant him this privilege would be to approve in advance any intervention Jurgen might wish to make in their marriage. Adams hired a Unitarian minister, and throughout the ceremony Pamela's parents, in the front pew, criticized his performance. "His voice is a little shaky," Adams heard Jurgen whisper. "Such a monotone," said Pamela's mother.

Now, on the phone, Jurgen's telling him the story of Abraham and Sarah, who survived hardships with unending faith and love and were able to conceive a child even after their bodies were withered and broken.

Whenever Jurgen preaches, he quotes liberally from a variety of sources. Like Pamela, he is proud of his German ancestry, and is particularly fond of Nietzsche and Hegel. He has misconstrued Nietzsche's Will to Power as "willpower" and erroneously paraphrases him in a Christian context. Hegel pops up in his apocalyptic sermons. "History's coming to an end," Jurgen shouts. "The Book of Revelation says so, the great Lutheran thinker Hegel says so."

Listening to him, Adams loses trust in narrative. In Jurgen's hands narrative is simply a form of typology, a chain of causality, leaving no room for accident. Adam was the forerunner of Moses who was the forerunner of Christ who became a scapegoat for all mankind. . . . Well, Adams thinks, you see the trouble that's gotten us into.

He has drawn enough jagged coastlines and isolated islands to be a firm believer in accident.

In sum, he does not get along with Pamela's father.

The only member of Pamela's family he enjoys is her uncle Otto. A rounder and a scoundrel, Otto is one of the richest men in Pennsylvania. He quit school in the fifth grade, learned sign-painting, and along with his father designed billboards all over the East Coast. When his father died, he discovered that the old man *owned* much of the East Coast, though he'd lived like a pauper all his life. Otto inherited so much land that the Army Corps of Engineers had to consult him each time they planned a project in the Delaware basin.

"You can't really own a piece of land," he once told

Adams. "It's there for anyone to sleep and piss on. Besides, my inheritance never stopped me from sinking to my proper level in life." With buckets of silver and buckets of gold he formed images up and down America's highways, meanwhile accumulating interest on his holdings—money he rarely touched. He didn't drink much before the age of fourteen, but "did quite a bit," he said, "after that." He preferred to live like his father and had no use for the rest of Pamela's family. "Tight-assed Lutheran Krauts," he called them.

Adams agreed, but did not want to upset Jurgen any more than the separation already had. He sounded old.

"It's all for the best, Jurgen. We were going in different directions. Pam's found a whole new career—"

"Don't go blaming Pammy for your oversights."

"We both made mistakes."

"Excuses won't wash with God, Sam. Marriage is a sacred institution."

"Jurgen, please, I want you to stop worrying about it. Let Pam and me work this out ourselves, all right? In the meantime, you take care of yourself."

"I'm fit as a fiddle. Don't change the subject."

Adams' family is easier. His mother and father divorced just after Kenny was born. She stays at home with migraines, he runs a miniature golf course on the outskirts of Red Cloud. When she wasn't in bed with pain, she was arguing with the old man in the clubhouse next to the eighteenth green. The final fairway led to a clown's face, sad as a frozen dinner, with pointed eyes and a grinning mouth. The tongue was a red slide up which the ball rolled into the hole located just behind the clown's uvula. Adams remembers sitting on the tongue, watching his parents threaten each other with putters.

Though neither is happy when he calls and tells them his troubles, they listen and forgive.

A note from Mayer: "Re our earlier conversation. Mr. Jordan has been under an intense emotional strain of late, factors having to do mainly with overwork. At my request, Mr. Carter has agreed to allow him some time off. You'll be happy to know that Mr. Jordan's problems are not serious. He is not a threat to you, nor has he ever been. I am satisfied you will not be bothered again."

Part Three

THE pleasure he took in naming his children is the same pleasure he feels in finishing a map. State names, county names, city names. The names of rivers, marshes, fjords. What the seas are called, the continents, the winds hushed deep in coves. The first name of a forest. The original word for a ridge. Irish, Icelandic, Nordic. Indian similes, Eskimo symbology, the nomenclature of the Vikings. Script (so ferociously ornate it reveals the cloistered monk's distrust of words), bold strokes (the explorer's hand), primitive type. German, Russian, French.

The world map of John Speede, 1626, revealing in the Southern Unknowne Land the County of Parrots, so named because of the "extraordinary and almost incredible bigness of those birds there."

Ptolemy, the father of design, advising, "We shall do well to keep the straight line."

Columbus wrote that the world resembles a woman's breast, terrestrial paradise flourishing at the spot that corresponds to the nipple.

Adams has mapped amazing ground. Six years ago, on a summer field trip to Mexico, he and his party lodged at a ranch thirty miles south of Mount Ciénega, an active volcano. Lava had altered the face of the landscape, diverting rivers, forcing villages to relocate, contaminating Sonora's water supply. Adams had been asked to make preliminary sketches for revised maps of the region.

A nearby university used the ranch for agricultural research, but graciously allowed the American party to stay in the main house. Adams' room overlooked the barn and the smell of rye grass and the chuffing of horses in their stalls reminded him of Red Cloud.

One night, unable to sleep, Mount Ciénega rumbling in the distance, he dressed and walked outside. The mosquitoes were thick; fallen berries snapped beneath his feet. Slapping the back of his neck he entered the barn. It was still. The animals were tense. He waded through the hay and was startled to see, in the corner, a thick white snake wrapped around a cow's hind legs, its mouth firmly attached to the udder. The terrified cow stared at the slats in the side of the barn.

Pamela has prepared cold zucchini and buttermilk soup. "I'm on a vegetarian diet," she says. "Did you know that for every sixteen pounds of soy and grain fed to cows, we only get one pound of beef? The Institute for Food and Development says eating meat is like driving a Cadillac."

Toby won't touch the food. Neither will Adams. Deidre is eating with a friend.

"I understand you've been saying some nasty things to your mother," Adams says.

"He called me an uncool bitch just before you got here."

"Is that why you came over?" Toby says. "To yell at me?"

"No. But I don't want you calling your mother names. Not to her face, and not behind her back."

"Bitch."

"Do you hear me?"

Toby mutters something else.

"I mean it, son."

Toby stands. "Bitch!" he shouts.

"If you call her that one more time—"

"How do you know I'm talking to her?"

"All right, is it me you're upset with?"

Toby sits.

"Is that it?"

He props his elbows on the table. "I'm not upset," he says. "And I'll do whatever I want."

"You'll do your homework."

"If I feel like it."

"You'll feel like it," Adams warns him, "after dinner."

"We're doing geography," Toby says. "It sucks. All those stupid maps."

"Your feelings toward me have been noted. But you're still going to have to do your homework."

Toby pushes himself away from the table. "I'll do whatever I want."

"Go to your room," Pamela tells him. "And stay there."

Toby leaves the kitchen.

Pamela smooths the tablecloth in front of her. "I don't know what to do with him. I've talked to a couple of doctors."

"He doesn't need to see a doctor. For God's sake, Pam, we just split up. It's bound to be confusing—"

"Poor man, he's become so boring boring boring."

"It needs to be discussed. You're like Fort Knox these days. I never see you, never hear from you."

"If it's the money—"

"To hell with the money."

"I can't deal with him, Sam. Last week he sat here throwing lighted matches at me."

"Lighted matches?"

"Let me try a doctor."

"All right," Adams concedes. "But on a trial basis. I want to know how he's coming, and if there are no good signs within a month, we do something else."

"Okay."

"Your family's always been quick to push the panic button."

"If you mean my father—"

"That's right. He'd have Toby in juvenile court. It's a wonder he hasn't locked Otto up."

"He *should* be. He's a drunk."

"He's not as bad as Jurgen thinks."

Pamela folds her arms. "He has too good a time."

Adams knocks on Toby's door.

"Come in."

Toby jounces on the side of the bed. Once. Twice. His shoulders drop, he slumps and places his elbows on his knees.

"What is it," Adams asks. He sits on Toby's American Bicentennial desk with the bald eagle decoupaged on top. The desk was a gift from Otto one Christmas—he had taken a sudden shine to the children.

Above the desk, a poster of a woman in a leopard-skin bikini, gazing provocatively from the crotch of a tree. She is famous, though Adams can't recall her name, acts in a television series and does commercials for a popular soft drink.

Toby's room is clean, almost empty.

"What's bothering you, Toby?"

"Nothing."

"Come on."

Toby jounces on the bed.

"Things have been pretty rough."

"I'll say."

"Let's talk about it."

"I don't want to."

"Would you rather talk to your mother?"

"No."

"Why are you giving her such a hard time?"

"I'm not."

"She said you threw matches at her."

Toby doesn't answer.

"It hasn't been easy on her, either, you know."

"I know."

"Well then, why don't you give her a break?"

"She's always busy."

"She's very talented."

"Does she hate you?"

Adams stands, smooths his pants. "No."

Toby jounces higher. "When you're married and you like each other, you fuck a lot, right?"

"Are you trying to shock me with your language, is that what you're trying to do?" He feels the leopard woman's eyes on him as he moves around the room. "Because if that's what you're trying to do, it won't work."

"Don't be an igno, Dad." Toby stops jouncing. "Everybody says it. But Mrs. Sorge, the principal, heard me and now I've got detention for a week."

"For saying—"

"Fuck."

"That's all?"

"No."

"What else?"

"We were on the playground."

"And?"

"I peed on a girl's shoes."

Adams resists an impulse to laugh. "You must like her a lot."

"Yeah." For a second Toby smiles, then his face hardens. "Mom wants to ground me."

"I think you deserve it, Toby."

"She can't stop me from doing what I want."

"She can take your money away from you and make you sit in your room."

"No she can't."

Adams believes him.

"She doesn't care what happens to me."

"You know that's not true, Toby."

"And she hates you. I can tell."

Maybe I should wrap a steel tube around his neck, pin him to a tree with wooden pegs.

When Toby was six he joined the Indian Y-Guides, a father-son organization sponsored by the YMCA. Adams went to meetings, wore a silly headband and feather, helped Toby make bulletin boards, letter holders, hot pads. (The leader of the "tribe," a retired fireman, nixed Adams' suggestion that they all make tom-toms—"too damn noisy.") In early December the Y-Guides took a bus to an abandoned state park, now overrun with weeds. The nights were cold, Toby cried, peed in his sleeping bag, lost both his shoes. He was never, after that weekend on the plains, a "joiner." Refused the Cub Scouts, church groups (shook Jurgen mightily), Little League. They would never explore together, father and son.

He mixes a Scotch, presses the suit he will wear tomorrow morning, removes the *Ixodes* from his pocket and places it on the nightstand next to his wallet. He sits in the dark, eating the ice, recalling happier days.

Alaska. He had joined a geological survey, exploring uninhabited regions in northern Birkin County. They had flown in by Piper Cub and landed, late at night, on a dirt road between water and ice. On the plane a graduate student from the University of Oklahoma, who'd done fieldwork the previous summer, suggested that each member of the survey take sulfur pills. "If you sweat sulfur, the insects'll leave you alone," he said, and passed around a Dopp Kit full of tablets. In the mountains the mosquitoes were big as birds, and more colorful.

Grizzly bears also posed a problem, especially in wooded areas where the snow was beginning to melt. To warn the bears of their approach the geologists draped cowbells around their equipment. One young man played Bob Dylan (badly) on the harmonica.

Hunters from Seattle and San Francisco shot caribou from helicopters at night. Adams couldn't see the sport in this but tried it one night, unsuccessfully, to see what it was like.

He was young. Just married. Endless vistas.

In 1978, when the focus had narrowed for him and he was very much a married man, seismologists began to question existing plans of the Izu Trench and the Okhotsk Abyssal Plain. The Plain, they felt, was perhaps twice as deep as previous calculations had indicated. In Tokyo, on his last assignment abroad, Adams met the Japanese cartographers who would accompany him to the coast. At a sushi dinner the day before they left, a man named Onu spoke of a recent survey he'd done at the foot of Mount Fuji. The survey had been interrupted by a manhunt in the foothills. A twenty-one-year-old Tokyo woman, who had recently broken her engagement to a young banker, was missing. A week later, police turned up not only her body but the badly decomposed bodies of six others, four male, two female. "Fuji has come to be known as Suicide Mountain," Onu said. The 6,250-acre Aokigahara woodland at Fuji was, Adams learned, the most popular spot for self-destruction in all of Japan. Annually, thirty to sixty people—businessmen, usually, or pregnant women disowned by their families—made a suicide pilgrimage to Fuji. "The forest is one of the most picturesque in Asia," Onu continued. "It has a sacred, gloomy aspect, and most of these people simply wander into the woods, lose themselves in the foliage, and starve. Their skeletons are often found under leaves." As he spoke he fingered prawns and gracefully scooped slivers of tuna into his mouth.

The following day Adams and his crew flew to the coast. From there they chartered the *Glomar Challenger* and sounded depth charges along the northern edge of the trench. Shrimp boats hovered near them all afternoon, waving their nets in the sun. The ship's captain, an American who'd spent the last eight years on the Sea of Japan, explained to Adams that American shipping was dying. "Can't compete with foreign prices," he said. He was returning to the United States next month to guide a ferry. "I can make more as a ferry pilot than I can as the captain of a ship." He showed Adams the radar system—a constantly changing, transparent map—and provided cheerful explanations of the ship's workings.

The crew drank beer, watched a school of sharks in the warmer waters of the continental slope, and compiled their charts. On the way in, early evening, they toasted the coastal lights and listened to a Japanese broadcast of the World Series.

Disappointed with the initial results of the mission, Adams remained in Japan for another four months, taking time off to visit other parts of the country. At Aokigahara, his access to the forest was limited by yet another manhunt: a party of schoolchildren had wandered away from their class picnic and had not been seen in two days. The police had reason to suspect that the children had lost themselves intentionally, to fulfill a suicide pact. When Adams expressed astonishment, a Japanese tourist assured him, "Japan, unfortunately, has one of the highest child suicide rates in the world. Our school system is very rigorous and many children succumb to the pressure."

In the forest Adams paused to rest in a small clearing. The wood's magnetic rocks confounded compass readings but he had kept his eye on a line of trees. He wiped his forehead with a handkerchief, relaced his shoes, and started to move on when he heard a rustling in the leaves. He paused. Again. Adams turned and crept toward the shade. There, kneeling in the dirt, were two little girls wearing checkered dresses. Their bangs were long. Adams crouched. One of the girls began to giggle. Her friend, startled at first, joined her. Adams sat back on his heels and watched the laughing little girls.

Deidre crying. "Toby hit me."

"Apologize to your sister."

"No," Toby says.

Adams sends them to bed.

All night, sniffles from their rooms. Adams gets up, feels his way along the wall. He winds up in the kitchen, annoyed that he cannot find his way around the house in the dark. In the field behind his yard two boys, bundled against the cold, light a Roman candle. The cardboard tube explodes, knocking the boys face down into the weeds. Before Adams can reach the back door, the boys leap up, apparently unharmed, and slice a path through the stickers. Adams calls his kids, feeds them ice cream and cakes. "What's wrong, Dad? What's the matter," Deidre asks, holding out her cone. "Can I have some more?"

. . .

When Pamela was pregnant with Toby, she craved foods that didn't exist. "Is there something that tastes the way furniture polish smells?" Adams made a meatloaf that nearly fit the bill, but nothing quite satisfied her and she moped around the house, miserable. To cheer her up, Adams bought an ottoman on which she could recline, and several cans of Lemon Pledge to polish it.

Yesterday Pamela arrived with a U-Haul for the ottoman and the oak wardrobe she had left behind. Adams is glad to have the furniture out, but the change is unsettling. He goes to Morty's early, orders a couple of beers. Bob arrives at eight-thirty and tunes his bass guitar. Before the first set begins, Bob addresses the band. "We were shit last week. Sam dragged on nearly every tune."

Pete and Denny turn to look at Adams.

" 'Dock of the Bay' saved us but let's tighten up, all right?"

There is something about guitars and cords and amps that changes a man. During the week Bob and Denny are polite businessmen, Pete a smooth announcer, but let them strap on a Fender or pick up a Gibson and they develop a slouch, mumble "Hey," and squint whether the room is smoky or not.

Tonight the combo will alternate sets with a punk band Morty has hired to appeal to the teenagers. Orphaned by Bullets, they're called. The drummer has blue hair.

"I wouldn't do that," he tells Adams. Adams is rubbing his cymbals with Brasso and a rag.

"It changes the molecular structure. Your cymbals turn into wax paper."

He's nineteen, pimpled, answers to Zig. His drums are plastic, transparent, flat as tables. A long extension cord connects his toms to an outlet behind the bar. The drums *ping* when hit, and reverberate for several seconds.

Adams' set looks clumsy next to the modern equipment. Zig gapes at Adams' snare. "Where's it plug in?" he says.

Pete is sitting at a table next to a short young girl. "Sam, this is Mary."

"Hi. I'm Sam."

"You're good. I heard you last week."

"Thanks."

"Mary goes to high school," Pete says, grinning. He offers her a cigarette. She says something about living on her own. It's not clear to Adams how she can rent an apartment or stay out late without her parents' consent.

"So, what do you do when you're not playing the drums?"

"I draw maps."

"Neat." Her T-shirt says RELAX. "You know what, I think we should have an adventure when you guys get off," she says. Her toes are painted red. "Buy some shit and go sleep on the moon."

"Time to swing," Pete says, tapping Adams' arm.

Adams follows him, takes his place behind the drums, and counts them into the first set. After ten minutes the band's in gear, they're relaxing, but the air remains charged, keeping the songs tight. The set moves nicely, and when they kick into "Dock of the Bay" they've never been better. Melody and rhythm work together like two bodies long accustomed to the steady timing of affection.

Orphaned by Bullets sounds a little like hash brown potatoes being shaken in a jar. Pete and Denny fall on each other with laughter, order extra Scotch-and-waters. Adams and Bob, gauging the crowd reaction, listen intently to the tunes. In the eighties, punk is the come-together shout, but Orphaned by Bullets' sound is unlike any variation of rock and roll Adams has ever heard. Each member of the band, dressed in gray plastic overalls with dabs of wild paint in his hair, seems to be playing a mathematical progression on his instrument unlike the progressions performed by his cohorts. They are hardly a band at all in the traditional sense of the word, but the young crowd, which had been perfunctorily polite during the combo's set, is eating it up.

"We can't compete for this audience," Adams tells Bob.

"You're right. I figure jazz—straight jazz. They'll think it's something new. Next set, we open with 'Take Five.' "

"These cats are great!" Pete shouts across the table.

"Shut up, Pete," says Bob.

Adams calls Jill from a pay phone near the kitchen. She had wanted to come tonight to hear him play, but Carter dumped a box of paperwork on her at quitting time.

"How's it going?" Adams asks.

"Slowly. Carter's up to something."

"Like what?"

"Can't tell. What he gave me is incomplete, but it's complicated, that much I can see."

"Does it involve more real estate?"

"Somehow. I got a feeling things'll be hopping in another month or two."

"Listen, I get off around two-thirty."

"Come by. I'll be up."

Jill's *est* terminology annoys him—she knows this and teases him with it—yet sometimes it's strangely accurate. The word "impact," for example, with its soft plosive *p*, reminding him of sitting on a plane, without peanuts or gum, a popping in his ears, a sudden descent. . . .

"How did your wife's leaving impact you?" she asked one night. He fell and fell.

"Are you ever uneasy, doing stuff for Carter?"

"No," she answers. "It's my job."

"Right. Balzac said 'The individual is not expected to be more scrupulous than the nation.' "

"I don't know about that. I just figure he's building his own karma. In the next life he'll come back as an old chamois in a car wash. I'll wipe my dipstick with him."

Adams enjoys hearing her talk late at night after playing at the club, delights in the gentle pressure of her head on his arm.

The second marriage, they say, is the one for love.

He strokes her hair.

The first, too.

The phone wakes him from a dream: perfume, silken clothes.

Jill hands him the receiver. "Hello?" he says.

"Par*um*-pum."

"Kenny?"

"What's up?"

"It's late. What's happened?"

"Nothing, man, just checking to see if you're still kicking."

"What time is it?"

"One."

"Three here." He should never have given Kenny Jill's number.

"Good news. I'm fixed."

"You are?"

"No more going broke. I'm fixed with a band now."

"Great." Jill turns over, asks him who it is. "My brother."

"What?"

"Nothing, Kenny. That's great."

"We're doing a shoot for MTV next week. Song

called 'Thoughts You Never Had.' Rock's tribute to Nancy Reagan."

"Gonna get rich."

"Damn straight."

"We're splitting the bill with a punk band now. They've got synthesized drums and a Linn drum machine."

"I hate that fuckin' Linn," Kenny says. "Glorified metronome."

"Goddamn tin can." Adams enjoys his brother.

As Kenny talks, Adams' dream comes back to him: he was swimming in a sea of women's clothes, with an erection like a wooden mast. Perfume sprayed his face. His body was heavy, sopping with the scent. He touches Jill's bare shoulder, leans back on the blue-striped pillow, and drifts away again, Kenny's voice a distant warning from shore.

No one, he thinks, properly appreciates the difficulty of beginning. He is entering coordinates into the computer. Latitude, longitude, the *Tome Pepsi* sign hanging by a nail on the wall, facing north, of that brown adobe bar in Ciudad Acuña, the river in south Texas where he lost his high school ring, all reduced to a set of binary numbers, neat, concise.

Caprice, he thinks, occupies much of the world's space.

A sign on the wall says, PROPER NAMES/DANGEROUS WORDS. The gallery is nearly empty. A series of pedestals in the center of the room support copper cylindrical tubes—he recognizes these as more sophisticated models of the equipment Pamela used to tinker with in the garage. Atop the copper tubes, attached with wires, striated plastic cylinders rotate slowly. Images appear inside the cylinders. In one, an image of Pamela, strands of her dark hair blowing violently across her forehead. As the cylinder turns she raises her arms. She is holding a camera. With a sardonic smile she snaps the viewer's picture. Then she lowers her arms and closes her eyes. Another cylinder reveals, bit by bit, a house frame, crossbeams and posts. As the cylinder turns the frame crumbles in a funnel of dust.

Most of the cylinders contain words. *Wirklichkeit* is here. So is Marriage, a vague, faded pink, floating as if underwater.

Pamela's other words:

Odyssey
Acceptance
Pageant
Stasis
Leftovers
Distant Warning
Thrombosis
Vertical Ruins

On the gallery walls, framed holographic images illuminated by black light: spectra of various lengths and intensities, silver, gold, and blue. Names of actors and politicians (Strom Thurmond, Veronica Lake), a more traditional collage reminiscent of Picasso.

The catalog says, "Saussure writes, 'In language there are only differences,' emphasizing the centrality of choice. A term's meaning is determined by a host of other terms not chosen. Ms. Adams' work renders dramatically this structuralist principle. Her words, free of referents as they are free of frames and museum walls, are tangible negations resisting interpretation. In representing only themselves, their meanings attached to words that the artist did not choose, they fill the gallery space, almost invisibly, with absence."

In the fall the valley turns green. Scholars and mystics have joined hands in attempts to explain why our seasons misbehave. Weathermen pepper our skies with balloons, diviners scratch the earth with sticks. Legends, and curious accounts in leather pouches found in the hollow of a tree, suggest that the valley was once a lake. Dogwood bloomed on its banks, peacocks danced in the hills.

Fishermen reported seeing water sprites, twinkling, no fatter than fingers, change into bulbous squashlike creatures in the middle of the night. What appeared to be falling leaves drifted slowly out over the lake, then turned into metal filings, which rained down hard upon the men. Nothing was safe. The shapeshifters smashed turtles, birds, trawlers, anything that settled on the lake.

On shore a chubby boy, an orphan, lived on the pumpkins of the fields. He longed to swim. As he had no family, the villagers assumed responsibility for him. They warned him of the danger in the water, but he seemed to have an intimate knowledge of the lake. He spoke of the colors at the bottom as though he'd been diving. Some people suggested that he came from the lake; after all, he had no family. Where *did* he come from?

One night, having informed the fishermen that he was tired of treading the earth, he jumped into the shallows and swam. From time to time the townsfolk saw him in the middle of the lake, riding a shaggy white buffalo. Eventually the boy wrenched a horn from the animal's head and tossed it ashore. A tree laden with heavy fruit sprang up where it landed. Next the boy surfaced gripping a black obelisk. The obelisk was slippery; often the boy lost his grip, but finally managed to fling it ashore. An artesian well burst forth, spraying water high into the air. The villagers danced beneath the spring, feasting on heavy fruit as the boy battled tumbleweeds, crates, panes of glass. Each time he hurled an opponent ashore it became, instantly, a source of beauty and health. The people were delighted.

Finally one creature remained—the mother squash, the biggest in the lake. The boy caught his breath, ate a chunk of pumpkin, submerged. He was underwater for hours. The lake boiled. Orange steam rose in patches off the water. The water began to blaze. Women from the village tossed ice into the deepest part. A mixture of blood—male and female, mother and son—hardened on the surface, burst into flames. It burned until the lake dried up. Afterwards there was no sign of the boy or the squash—just a salt deposit, as if from giant tears. For years boiling rain seared the dogwoods in the valley. The grass dried up in summer.

He turns out the light. "Good night," he says.

"Daddy?"

"Yes?"

"That was neat. Will you tell us another story tomorrow night?"

"Sure. Go to sleep now."

He sits up with a drink, then falls asleep in his chair and dreams about the valley he had mentioned in the children's story. When he wakes up he goes to his drafting table and on a thin sheet of paper tries to recall the dream: "Each morning before the valley is awake the little girls escape. Their curtains blow through windows, like blouses opening. They're out to catch the fathers.

"The fathers have not been home all night. Their coats are creased, faces rough with stubble. Before the sky is light they've ordered bacon, eggs, toast and jelly, waffles, bagels with cream cheese. In the alley, doors X-ed with boards echo the children's hisses, shadows dart across the bricks. When the fathers leave the diner, they discover that their cars have been pushed down the street and rest, engines smoking, in a pile.

"It matters, our life with women, how we hurt them if we see them, but the little girls have clearly had enough."

A picnic with the kids in the car beneath an overpass.

"This is great," Deidre says, pulling thick waxed paper away from a fat pimiento sandwich.

He had simply pulled off the road because he knew it would surprise them, and they are pleased whenever you surprise them.

"Put the Coke on the dash," he says. "You'll spill it."

Deidre spills it trying to put it on the dash. Apologies. Kleenex. Toby turns the radio on as high as it will go. Elvis Costello singing "Watching the Detectives."

"We can do without that," Adams says, turning the radio down. "I wanted to ask you—Toby, be careful." Pulling over was not a good idea. "Okay, leave it, I'll get it later. I wanted to ask you how you're getting along now. It's been a while since you moved into the new house. Do you like it all right? Is everything okay?"

A Jeno's Pizza truck roars by, shaking the car. The kids eat in silence. They've learned the game. Keep quiet. Don't rat on Mom. When the adults are acting funny, stay out of their way.

"I just want to know if you're happy," Adams says, brushing crumbs from the seat. He misses being able to surprise them. When they were very young, a stray cat came into the backyard. Pamela fed it every evening and they loved to watch it. Deidre was wild with new expressions—a dozen every day, it seemed—and "cat" was one of her favorite discoveries. Just for fun Adams started referring to the stray as a "catezoidal object." The kids laughed uproariously, impressed that you could call a thing more than one name, or twist words around to make them sound funny. Now that he sees Toby and Deidre only on weekends he has to schedule their time wisely. Surprise has gone out of their Saturdays. "Things haven't been the same, I know," Adams says.

Toby replies, "You can say that again."

"Well, tell me about it. How does it make you feel? What can I do for you?"

"Buy me a sheep," Deidre says.

"Shut up," Toby says.

"*You* shut up."

"Would you like to stay with me more? Not just on weekends, but maybe during the week sometimes?"

"I don't know," Toby says. He's been seeing a psychologist once a week. The man, he says, "sucks."

"Could we stay up late and watch TV?"

"Not on school nights."

"Please, Dad."

"No. Not on school nights. You know better than that."

"It's no fun," Toby says, "when you have to plan things."

"I know. Do you have fun with Mom? Does she spend enough time with you?"

Silence. Well, it was a loaded question.

"I know she's busy a lot."

"She's all right," Toby says.

Adams thinks she's frightening. Lately, to give her "Dangerous Words" more depth, she's been reading Wittgenstein. When he picked up the children, she read him the opening paragraph of *The Brown Book*: "Augustine, in describing his learning of language, says that he was taught to speak by learning the names of things. It is clear that whoever says this has in mind the way a child learns such words as 'man,' 'sugar,' 'table,' etc. He does not primarily think of such words as 'today,' 'not,' 'perhaps.' "

She also showed him a David Hockney photograph, a woman in a thin lace blouse, tousled hair, one arm thrown languorously over her head, hand brushing her cheek. The photograph was pieced together from several Polaroids so that the woman had two noses, three eyes, two mouths. A hand in four parts. The overall effect was of movement, of seeing a two-dimensional image from several angles at once. "Cubist photography," Pamela said. "That one," pointing to the woman, "resembles Picasso's Marie-Thérèse series. *The Red Armchair*. Remember, I showed you?"

Adams does not remember.

Her house must be full of surprises: face parts, altered bodies, words hung like wet towels from the shower rod, drying in the sink, smuggled under pillows. Adams fears boring his children.

"I know what," he says. "Would you like to come to the club some night and hear me play the drums?"

"Yeah!" Deidre says. Toby shrugs.

"You haven't heard me play in a long time."

A Ryder rental truck swooshes by on the highway.

"Didn't you have fun," Adams asks.

"Yes," they answer at once, the practiced response.

"I don't think Toby likes me," says Jill, delightfully naked, closing the bedroom door. The furniture seems to change temperature whenever she spends the night.

"He doesn't like anybody," Adams answers. "I'm hoping he'll outgrow it."

He is on his back on top of the sheet. She leans over him, touches the top of his ear with her lips. "You're a good man," she says.

"I don't want to be a good man."

"Show me."

He catches the small of her back with his arm and rolls her over on top of him so that she is facing the ceiling, her shoulders resting against his chest. With his hands he warms her stomach. She bends her knees, locks her legs on either side of his hips, and lifting her arms over her head, sends her fingers through his hair.

. . .

Pamela phones. "I hear you have a new friend."

"Yes."

"Listen, Toby took the ledgers and financial records from your closet. I found them in his room yesterday. He had your canceled checks spread out on the bed. He said he's auditing you for a political science project. Claims you owe five hundred dollars in back taxes."

The figure's a little high, Adams thinks. "I'll come by tomorrow," he says.

"All right. One more thing, Sam. I've hired a divorce lawyer."

"Oh?"

"Can we not be messy about this?"

"No problem," Adams says.

City code (written): One parking space/four theater seats. Theaters best located in suburbs. Commuters generally do not return to the downtown area at night for pleasure after leaving the downtown area after work. Four- to six-screen theater complexes, corporately managed (AMC, Loews, etc.) to be encouraged for zoning purposes (i.e., limit entertainment space as much as possible).

Adams recalls the wide, balconied theaters of his youth, stone pillars on either side of the screen.

City code (unwritten): Fast-food franchises generally discouraged for the present. Reasons cited: (1)

glut (2) cash flow out of the community. Records indicate that seventy-four percent of expenditures at a single McDonald's restaurant flow out of the community (food and paper from the corporation, rent paid to the corporation, advertising, accountants, lawyers).

City code (revised, S. Adams): Freeway overpasses with more than forty percent curvature to be dislodged by giant cranes and placed, unanchored, on the ground in reversed position, to serve as bases for rocking horses roughly the size of three-story buildings. Ancient cannon (howitzers, etc.) to be removed from military museums and welded together as superstructure for legs, tails, heavily maned necks. Clouds snagged by oversized cloth nets stretched between helicopters to be used for padding in Astroturf-and-leather saddles. Redbud trees bundled together and tied are to be placed on the horses' noses: *blazing nostrils.* In addition, cypress trees to be imported from states with large rivers, sculpted to resemble butterflies, birds, painted white, gold, blue, and suspended mobile-like from cranes around the horses.

Deidre dressed for dance rehearsal. In her grass skirt and cap she looks like a little hut. "Why don't you tell me what happened?" Adams says.

"Well, we were in David's yard—"

"David is the little boy. . . ?"

"Next door. His daddy took down his swing set." She stops, as though she's made her point.

"And?"

"He's really mean. He doesn't want David to have any fun."

"Okay, so then what happened?"

"So then . . . we were in David's yard, okay? And his daddy took down his swing set. And there was this metal bar, you know, that used to be part of the swing set, and I picked it up and started throwing it in the air like a baton, okay? And I wasn't throwing it high, like he said I did, and it came down on David's head."

"How badly was he cut?"

"I didn't see him bleeding or anything, but five minutes later David's dad comes over here yelling at me like I'm some kind of wookie or something."

"They had to take him to the emergency room," Pamela says.

"Has this sort of thing happened before, Deidre?"

"No. What do you mean?"

"Well, apparently David's father says the other kids are afraid of you."

"That's 'cause they're really really dumb. I liked it better where we lived before."

"What have you been doing?"

"*Nothing.*"

"Tell your father about the Crisco," Pamela says.

"Oh, that's stupid."

Adams says, "What about the Crisco?"

"I was with Stephanie in her kitchen—"

"Stephanie is eighteen months old," Pamela adds.

"And I thought it would be funny to put Crisco on her face to make her look like a clown."

"Stephanie was covered with Crisco head to toe," Pamela says.

Adams laughs.

"It's not funny, Sam."

"You had me thinking she was terrorizing everybody."

"I never said that. That was Mr. Doyle, David's father."

"He's really mean," Deidre says.

"He had no right to yell at her. I'll punish my own kids the way I see fit," Pamela says.

"*Ma*-ma."

"All right," Adams says. "I'll take you to dance class. And tomorrow I want you to apologize to David and his father."

"It was an accident!"

"You're sorry it happened, aren't you? And if you haven't apologized to Stephanie's mother, I think you should do that too."

"And to Stephanie?"

"Yes, and to Stephanie."

"She won't understand, Dad."

"Well, you'll teach her. Now get your stuff." He slaps her bottom.

Pamela offers him a drink. "I'm not home enough, Sam. I know that's part of the problem." In addition to her work, she's now involved on a volunteer basis with a social group called Women Against Poverty. On Tuesday nights she counsels battered wives, distributes food to women whose food stamps have been rescinded by federal cuts, and helps uneducated single mothers put together résumés and fill out job applications.

"You should see these women when they realize how easy it is to fill out a job application. They think their problems are over. Of course they're just beginning. I don't know how much good we do. Sometimes I think we're getting their hopes up for nothing. But I'm teaching them art. I've put these cutouts on the wall, like Matisse dancers, and we talk about color and proportion. Most of them don't care, but it takes their minds off their children and their boyfriends and their bad checks."

"Don't worry about the kids. We'll work things out."

Deidre is ready to go. Adams drops her off at class, circles back, and has a talk with Mr. Doyle, a nervous man who turns out to be friendly and reasonable.

"I'm sorry if I upset your wife," he says.

"Understandable. And you probably did Deidre some good. David's all right?"

"He's going to be fine."

Fathers being fatherly.

Adams offers to pay David's medical costs; Mr. Doyle politely declines.

Adams drives to the women's shelter with a bottle of champagne. "To celebrate your work. And the end of the hostilities with Mr. Doyle," he says.

The shelter is temporarily located in a vast warehouse, no private alcoves, and he feels embarrassed standing nicely dressed among crying women and children, holding a chilled bottle of Moët et Chandon.

"That's really sweet of you, Sam. Can you leave it in my car?" She hands him her keys and leads a mixed group of children—black, Chicano, Asian—toward a corner of the room. One of the boys repeats to himself in a deep, affected voice, "I worked late last night, worked late tonight, and I'm fed up, do you hear me, I've had it up to here." Loudly buzzing yellow lights glare from the rafters of the building, the gray metal walls are covered with cardboard figures holding hands and dancing in circles. Folding chairs and cots fill the space in the center of the room; on the sides, seven or eight portable freezers.

Adams follows Pamela, jangling her car keys. "Why don't you just come over when you get through tonight?" For some reason—perhaps because Mr. Doyle was so nice—he feels gracious and forgiving this evening.

"I'm going to be here awhile."

"How long?" He bumps into a pregnant woman with very thin legs and arms.

"I don't know, Sam. I'm just not up for it, okay? It was very sweet of you, but . . ."

"Okay, okay." He is jealous of the crowded shelter, of her purpose here.

She squats beside a woman with long curly hair. The woman is seated on the concrete floor.

"How you doing, Angela," Pamela asks.

Angela's left wrist is in a cast. "I haven't changed my mind," she says. Her tongue is cut.

"Please, Angela."

"Where did they park my car?"

"Stay with us, at least for tonight."

"I've got to see him again!" Angela starts to cry.

Pamela looks up at Adams: condemnation, fear, affection? He'd like to squeeze her shoulder reassuringly but knows she might consider it, at this moment, a hostile gesture.

City of Women Alone, Street of the Listener, Avenue of Lost Children. Come back. Return. So this is where we are.

Part Four

IN a dream Pamela mails him a plate. The Dutch are always giving plates. Ceramic plates, wooden plates, clay plates. Generally a hand-painted scene appears in the center of the plate, and around the rim an aphorism: "Happy the Soul Who Trusts in God" or "Coal Remains in the Hills." A distinct feature of the plates is that they often are addressed to brothers and sisters. Husbands and wives sometimes paint affectionate names on one another's plates, such as "Gimp" or "Woodchip." In Adams' dream the plate arrives wrapped in paper. He cuts the tape. When he removes the last shred of wrapping, he is astonished. In the middle of the plate a hag, like the witch in *Hansel and Gretel*, leans on a cane. Written in German script on the rim: "Good Morning, Cousin Snitch, You Kissed the Mouth for Nothing, didn't You?"

At the dance hall he drinks beer and eats sausage. Jill does the polka with a barrel-chested man in long pants and suspenders while Adams taps out a beat on a wooden table to the fiddle. He's thinking of all the dances in all the halls he ever attended with Pamela, but the people at the table with him raise their mugs and laugh heartily, and he can't help but feel good. Jill takes his hand and drags him onto the dance floor. It is covered with sawdust, and when she swirls, tiny wooden slivers lift into the air like snow and settle in her hair.

Watching her, Adams feels happy.

"Let's get our fortunes told," Jill urges him.

"I'm enjoying myself here."

"Come on, it'll be fun."

Rosa's in the middle of a séance when they arrive. "Come in, come in," an old woman whispers through the screen door. They sit on the floor behind a row of women, all of whom are holding hands.

Adams watches Rosa. She might have been attractive once, but years of tension have tightened the skin around her mouth. In the dim light her age shows—she must be in her sixties. The way she rotates her jaw as she slips into a trance is repulsive, and he looks away. Through the front screen he sees boys banging cans behind the cemetery. One of them pulls a frayed head of lettuce from a pile of garbage and they begin to toss it like a football. Outside it's getting dark and a cool breeze moves through the room.

The spirit that is speaking through Rosa, fluttering candles she has placed in small dishes on the floor, runs out of things to say and begins recommending her spaghetti. She comes out of her trance.

"Let's take a break," she says. "There's strawberries and cream in the kitchen."

She's delighted to see Adams and asks about the children. He introduces her to Jill, who's wholly taken with the scene. "How did you get into this?"

"I started out with a crystal ball, but if you get someone with a clouded past the ball will literally cloud up. You can't hide it from the client. It's very embarrassing. I prefer to let people experience their own pasts directly, and that's what we're going to do next. Grab some strawberries and join us."

Adams is uneasy but Jill wants to stay. He sits on the floor next to her. "Nadine." Rosa gestures to a woman with swollen ankles. "You've regressed with me several times. What have you been?"

"I grew cabbages in Italy during the Dark Ages. I sank with Atlantis."

She lies on the floor in front of Rosa and folds her arms over her abdomen. Her ankles are extraordinarily thick; her heels just touch the ground. Rosa leans over her. "Close your eyes," she says. "Breathe slowly."

Nadine's ankles pulse as if something were trying to hatch from them.

Rosa says softly, "There's a warmth like water in your stomach, calming every muscle. It fills your chest like foam, washes into your neck and shoulders."

Nadine appears to be asleep.

"Now then, I want you to take a little journey with me. Imagine yourself in a forest by a creek. Tell me what you see."

"I see a lizard on a rock. I see the sun."

"Good, good. What else?"

"Arrowheads in the dirt, sunflowers in tall grass, butterflies . . ."

"You're high in the air over a forest. When I count to three, you'll float slowly down until your feet touch the ground. And when they do, you'll find yourself in the past. One, two, three. Where are you, Nadine?"

The woman writhes on the floor. "It's hot," she says.

"Do you know where you are?"

"No . . . no, I don't know where I am."

"What are you wearing?"

"Black and white stripes."

"Is it a dress?"

"Skin. Animal skin."

Rosa nods. "Describe what you see."

She lived in an African village by an antelope herd and a pond, until one day she ran from her tribe. She'd been promised to a warrior whom she didn't want to marry. The tribal elders found her hiding behind a date palm, bound her to a stake, and tortured her with hot sticks until she agreed to accept the warrior. The wedding night passed pleasantly enough, despite the burns on her back.

Rosa counts Nadine out of her relaxed state. She smiles like a coed who's just passed an anthropology exam.

. . .

Jill is a Mexican peasant with callused feet and a swollen belly. For a few pesos each night she sweeps the streets of the city, smiling up at the candles in the rich folks' homes. Rosa advances her in years to her marriage, middle age, and death. Her husband dies young, her son becomes a farmer. She lives her late years in a convalescent home, attended by nuns.

Now it's Adams' turn. Because he's so self-conscious, Rosa takes a long time to relax him.

"Where are you," he hears her ask.

"I don't know." His hands feel weightless. "I'm moving." His mind supplies no image. "It's like I'm underwater."

"You're underwater, then?"

"Yes, I'm in a river." The image still isn't clear and Rosa's questions only bother him. Hard balls of mud slap his crotch. He feels this rather than sees it: his nerves move ahead of his mind. He bounces off a barge and tumbles to the bottom of the river. Muddy dregs sweep into his mouth.

"Where are you?"

"I don't know," he says.

The sky turns bright as cellophane. On a pine bridge above him two white deer chase each other. Dirt from their hooves sifts through a space between the boards and peppers his face.

Angry female voices mingle in the air above a wooden house. In a room full of rifles a white-haired man reads a map.

"I can't read," he tells Rosa.

"Move yourself forward in time," she suggests. "Where are you?"

"In town." He's carried the mud with him. His clothes are spattered. The streets are little more than damp ruts, and dirty geese straggle across them.

"What do you see?"

Rain barrels, wagon wheels, a tobacconist. "I'm standing in a hotel lobby," he says.

"Are you waiting for someone?"

"No. I don't know anyone."

A diamond-blue horsefly orbits a kerosene lamp.

"What's your name?"

"I don't know. The hotel looks full."

"Are you the clerk?"

"I can't read the register."

He turns on the television, hoping to run across Pavarotti again. Instead, PBS is airing a layman's guide to the universe hosted by Peter Ustinov, who looks a great deal like Pavarotti but without the mole. Ustinov holds up two billiard balls and rolls them across a curved table with a grid painted on it—a demonstration of what happens to matter when it encounters a black hole. The balls are sucked down a pipe in one corner of the table.

The weekend: *Superman III* with the kids. Superman, under the influence of not-quite-Kryptonite, has gone on a whiskey binge. The hero in him struggles to regain control of his mind, and in an urban scrapyard the two halves of his personality fight it out. Clark Kent, representing all that is pure within him, falls onto a conveyor belt, knocked silly by the unkempt superhero.

Deidre asks, "Why are they both on the screen at the same time?"

Adams explains split personality.

"That's stupid," Deidre says.

At home, she helps him peel shrimp. Toby, with exaggerated kindness, offers to mix him a Scotch-and-soda.

"Where'd you learn to mix drinks?" Adams asks.

"Mom had a party a couple of weeks ago. She taught me."

"Oh? Who was at the party?"

"Painters, mostly. They talked real loud and dressed funny." Toby twists his face, trying to be sullen, but obviously he's in a talkative mood tonight. "I liked being bartender. The women said I was cute and made a big fuss, which was gross, but two of them asked me to fix the zippers on their dresses."

"Yeah, Toby wanted to take their dresses off," Deidre says, tossing shrimp into a pot of boiling water.

"I did not." Toby walks off to make the drink.

Deidre asks, "Why don't you have a party, Daddy?"

"I might, someday."

"Can we come?"

"Sure." He can't imagine whom he'd invite.

"I want to be the bartender next time," Deidre says. "I'll help the men fix their ties."

Adams adds lemon and celery to the shrimp and covers the pot. He walks into the den, where Toby is standing, staring disconsolately at the drink he has mixed.

"What's the matter?"

"I don't know if I added enough soda."

Adams takes the drink. "Toby, what is it?"

Toby jounces on the couch. "You're not going to like it."

"Try me."

"All right." He assumes an innocent expression. "I want to know why you and Mom stopped fucking."

"Toby . . ."

"I want to know why. Did you get tired of her?"

"Toby, we were getting along so well. Don't spoil it, please."

"I was watching these guys at Mom's party. They bragged about their work and acted stupid in front of these stupid women, and I know what was going on, they all wanted to fuck each other, the men and the women too, moving around each other like Muhammad Ali or something, waiting for the best shot. Mom was doing it too. Acting stupid every time she talked to a stupid guy."

Adams shrugs. "Men and women are attracted to one another for very good reasons," he says.

"Like what?"

"Like what, well, haven't you ever noticed a pretty girl at school and she smells good and she's very nice, but for some reason you don't get along with her? You don't know why, but you're just not interested in getting to know her? On the other hand, you meet a girl who's not so pretty but you kind of like her—"

"I don't like *anybody* in my class," Deidre says. "None of them know how to draw except me, and Mrs. Collins says we're the most obnoxious kids she's ever had."

"Or like your friends," Adams continues. "There are certain guys you like to hang around with—"

"I'm talking about fucking," Toby says.

"It's no different."

"What's fucking?" Deidre asks.

"Honey, please."

"Tell me."

"It's when a man and a woman get naked with each other," Toby shouts. Deidre's eyes grow big and she glances, frightened, at Adams, wondering if Toby's in trouble, or if she's in trouble, or if maybe Adams himself is in trouble.

"Women'll fuck anybody," Toby says.

"That's not true. It's especially not true of your mother."

"She was acting so stupid."

"That's called flirting. People do it because it's fun. It doesn't always lead to making love. It's like a game. Most of the time it doesn't mean anything."

"Sometimes it does."

"Sometimes. But people make choices. And people like your mother and me . . . well, we make responsible choices." He sips his drink. "Most of the time. Anyway, it's natural for you to be confused about all this, but believe me, it's not as crazy as you think. There were reasons your mother married me and not someone else." He pauses. "Just as there were reasons the marriage ended when it did." He hopes Toby won't ask him for the reasons. "What do you know about making love?" he says.

"I know how it's done."

"Do you want to talk about it?"

"No."

"Let me know when you do, all right?"

Toby nods.

Deidre is still at sea. Adams scratches her head. "Put the sauce on the shrimp, all right?"

"Sam, I'd like you to meet the Honorable Frederick Palmer, congressman from the tenth district."

"Pleased to meet you," Adams says.

Palmer is wearing a red string tie.

Carter takes them to an Italian restaurant, where he and Palmer discuss a water control project. Adams does not follow the conversation closely; it's clear he's not meant to.

"I'm being purposely vague," the congressman tells him, "because I don't want to confuse the issue."

Back in the office, Carter pulls Adams aside. "Palmer's going to help us with our next project. What

I'd like from you is a detailed map of the following region." He hands Adams a set of coordinates. "Thursday, hmm? Oh, and Sam, Vox has the W-2 forms in his office. When you pick yours up, sign for it, all right? There's been some hanky-panky with the records and we're trying to be more accurate."

"What kind of hanky-panky?" Adams asks.

Carter looks around. "Some cash is missing from the political action fund."

"Mallow?"

Carter shakes his head. "There's some other stuff, too. Just sign your name so we know you got your forms."

The women's shelter has moved to a permanent location, a gray two-story house wedged cozily among three giant cedars in one of the oldest neighborhoods in town. The grass is neatly mowed. Kids play tag between bashed-in-looking cars parked in the drive. A woman in a long skirt is sitting on the wooden porch in a rocker reading "The Cow Jumped Over the Moon" to a little girl nearly asleep on her lap.

"Hi. I'm Valerie."

"Valerie. Pam nearly through?"

"I don't know. I think they're reading poems."

Cicadas throb in the cedars. Lamplight falls through the lace curtains onto Valerie, who, Adams sees, is wearing a splint on her right arm.

He pokes his head in the door. A television, black-and-white, sound off, sits on a crumpled shower curtain in a corner of the living room. A circle of wooden chairs spotted with green paint. A chipped and dusty glass chandelier. On the walls (the same pale green as the spots on the chairs) Pamela's Matisse-figures playfully chase one another all the way up to the ceiling. In the stairwell one of the cardboard figures has come partially untaped and appears to have placed its feet on the carpeted stairs.

A woman clears dirty dishes and coffee cups from a poorly varnished table. Pamela motions for him to come in and shut the door. Most of the women are young—some in their early teens—and with children. A few are cut and bruised, made up heavily to hide the marks, but the rest seem healthy, in good spirits. A little tired perhaps. Cynical jokes.

A thickset lady next to Pamela picks up a paperback book and reads Wallace Stevens' "Anecdote of the Jar."

Only three or four women are listening, and all agree they don't understand that one.

"You're right, let's try another," the lady says, and chooses Emily Dickinson:

> I saw no way—the Heavens were stitched—
> I felt the Columns close—
> The Earth reversed the Hemispheres—
> I touched the Universe—
>
> And back it slid—and I alone—
> A Speck upon a Ball—

Went out upon Circumference—
Beyond the Dip of Bell—

"That's pretty," one woman says faintly, gazing out the window. Another turns up the sound on the television.

Pamela touches Adams' arm. "They don't need me anymore tonight. I'll just be a minute." She hugs several of the women (one flinches; "I'm sorry," Pamela says, gingerly rubbing the woman's ribs), straightens their hair, and accompanies Adams out the door. The little girl who was resting on Valerie's lap now stands in the front yard while Valerie pulls off her shorts and lays them in the grass.

"Diarrhea," Valerie says.

The little girl stares imperturbably at the cars passing on the street, as if this were just one more thing that has happened in her life.

"If you throw any more wild parties for your artist friends, I'm going to fight for custody," he announces with some degree of pleasure.

Pamela, stunned, lifts her glass of Riesling. "I don't think we should use the children to spy on each other."

"Who's spying. Toby felt bad and he let it out, that's all."

"So what are you telling me, Sam? I can't have people over?"

"I'm not in a position to tell you—"

"You're certainly not."

"But I won't have the children exposed to anything before they're ready."

"Unfit mother, is that it?"

"It's the crowd you're in with. Painters with their flies open—"

"Don't say another word, Sam. If you've got some horrible stereotyped image of artists, that's your problem, not mine. You don't know my friends. It's pretty damned impertinent of you to pass judgment."

"I know what Toby told me."

"He's a child. He doesn't understand—"

"That's my point." He gets up, leaving money for the bill.

"Don't walk out on me, Sam. This is not some goddamn movie where you can pull a stunt like that."

"Don't raise your voice to me."

"Here, take your money," she says, "I can pay for my own."

Elgin Creek is at its deepest in the area that Carter wants mapped. No one knows who owns the land. The county's contesting the claims of three families.

Adams puts his work aside for the afternoon, drives out to Deerbridge Road. He parks the car on a flat grassy spot next to a dirt path, gets out, slides down a brambly slope to the creek. Mimosa fuzz circles slowly in the air. He can hear the water but cannot see it through the bushy weeds. Finally he clears a path to the bank. The creek is green. Low. Swirling wildflowers and pebbles. Adams slaps mosquitoes from his neck, dabs his face with a handkerchief.

Absurd to worry about water control here.

A broken bottle of ink on the floor beneath his drafting table.

Deidre stands in the kitchen doorway.

"What happened?" he asks.

"It broke."

"I can see that. How?"

"I don't know."

For the first time in years he feels like spanking his child. "Did you break it?" he says.

"No."

Her first direct answer.

"Did Toby break it?"

She withdraws into the kitchen. Toby is sitting at the table, reading the morning paper. "There's an article on Mom's show."

"Did you break my bottle of ink?"

Toby looks at Deidre.

"I want you to stop using Deidre as a shield."

"What do you mean?"

"I mean I don't care who broke the ink. But if you've got your sister covering for you, I'm going to be very upset. Now, what's it going to be?"

Toby stares at the paper.

"Grown-ups admit their mistakes."

"Oh, yeah?" Toby stands behind his chair. "Do you admit you made a mistake when you let Mom leave?"

"I've made a lot of mistakes," Adams says. He turns to Deidre. "Did he tell you to lie for him?"

She glances at Toby.

"It's all right, honey. You can tell me."

She lifts her fingers to her lips. "He told me never get him in trouble."

"Do you know how to make toast and eggs," he asks. She nods. "All right, start the toast and eggs while I have a talk with your brother. I'll be in to help you in a minute." He leads Toby to the back porch. A cool spring morning. A wisp of fog in the air.

"I'm disappointed in you, Toby."

"I don't want to hear this shit."

"Well, you're going to. What bothers me is the way you treat your sister. If you want to hate your mother and me, that's fine. We're big people, we can take it. But you're bigger and stronger than Deidre, you know? I love you both, but so help me, Toby, if you frighten her or intimidate her in any way, you're going to wish you had a different father. Do you understand?"

Toby nods, his face bright red.

"Now let's eat some breakfast."

Adams tells Pamela he's going to stop paying for Toby's visits to the doctor.

"But he's getting better."

"He's getting subtler. He'll outgrow this phase or

he won't, but the doctor's not going to make a bit of difference."

"Sam, I don't know how to handle him."

"Neither do I. It's time we learned."

Rosa's sitting in the cemetery beneath a cottonwood tree. As Adams walks by on his way home from the library, she offers him an egg salad sandwich.

"Do you often picnic in the graveyard," he asks.

"Why not? It's pleasant, quiet. I've also got some Ruffles and a can of Tab."

He takes some potato chips.

"What'd you think about the other night?"

"It was interesting. I don't believe in past lives, though."

"The experience is what's important. Do you know Greek plays? Remember the Oracle at Delphi? The Greeks really believed she had divine power. Then some scholar comes along and says, 'Nah, it was a crazy old woman inhaling sulfur fumes from a crack in the earth.' The fumes changed her voice, see, so it sounded like some other being had taken hold of her. And she was eating hallucinogens from the plants, which made her sound mystical. I say, what the hell's the difference? The experience is the same."

"There's a big difference," Adams says. "It's important to know where you stand."

"Ahhh." Rosa waves her hand. "How're your kids?"

"Fine. They really enjoyed having their fortunes told."

"Your little boy's got a lot of hostility, you know?"

"Yes."

"Was he born in a leap year?"

Adams is astonished.

"Saw it right away. He's not at home with himself. He tries to keep up but he's like a slow watch. His sense of timing's been off from the start. He wants to be older than he is, and it crushes him that he's so far behind."

"I wish it were as simple as that."

"Believe me."

"Maybe I do."

"More chips?"

"No thanks."

"Well, drop by sometime. The dead don't say all that much."

Jordan is back at work, conciliatory, cheerful, refreshed. He insists on treating Adams to lunch. Jill comes along. She was questioned this morning about the missing money, as was Adams a week earlier. Routine, the accountant says, we're checking everybody. Jordan forgets his wallet and Adams ends up spending forty-three dollars.

Carter tells him, "Things'll calm down once this latest deal goes through. Ever been to Greenland?"

"No."

"I don't know if we can swing it, but Comtex has some interests up there. Word has it they're dissatisfied with the base maps Tobin and Muldrow have given them. Want their own, firsthand. Would you like me to check into it for you?"

"Wonderful, yes."

Adams waiting for the kids. Pamela reading into a tape recorder ("I have to prepare a lecture on art and politics for this little gallery downtown") a passage from Wittgenstein's *Remarks on Colour*: " 'White water is inconceivable.' That means we cannot describe (e.g. paint) how something white and clear would look, and that means: we don't know what description, portrayal these words demand of us."

"Hence," Pamela says into the recorder, "Dangerous words. No, scratch that. Let's see. Color. What can we say about color? Well, all right, for one thing, color is temporal—not like words on a page where it takes two minutes or whatever to read a paragraph. But Time, as in *the tenor of the times* or *the latter days of the twentieth century*, fixes color and dictates color choices. A silly example—get a better one later—say I'm working on a portrait. I pause for lunch and read about the deployment of medium-range missiles in Western Europe and I think about the end of the world and my mind trips back to the passage from Revelation that my father forced-fed me every night, about the moon turning blood-red. So when I return to the portrait, I mix a little extra red into the skin color. Temporality has chosen the color for me because I live in a tragic, temporal world."

Sometimes Adams sees colors when the band's in the middle of a set. It's as if there were a thin film of tinted water on the drums; when he taps them with a stick, sheets of blue-green, ruby, and yellow shimmer in the air.

"So much of modern art," Pamela continues, "has no philosophical basis. It's aimless and irresponsible, like the country. As such, it's an accurate barometer of the country. But every choice of color and form is a moral choice. We discriminate, one instead of another. That's why my art and my political consciousness are developing hand in hand, why the nuclear threat affects the way I draw a line."

According to a front-page story in the *Elgin Observer*, the Honorable Frederick Palmer, congressional leader of the tenth district, has secured funds from the Bureau of Reclamation to build a dam on the north bend of Elgin Creek for the purposes of flood control.

Adams checks the records: Elgin Creek has never flooded. Carter and Palmer have figured out a way to make a profit on the dam, and have government funds to pay for it.

He'll press harder for Greenland.

"Only one man I ever met had good reason for owning the land he did," Otto tells Adams on the phone. The connection is weak, since Otto lives in the mountains of Pennsylvania where telephone linemen seldom service equipment. One of the richest men in the state, he chooses to live in a one-room wooden cabin full of squirrel shit and mice. "When I worked as a landman, we scouted ranchers to see if they were willing to sell mineral rights to their property, then we looked for oil and gas. One time I visited this old man in western Kentucky. He owned a bunch of woods down there, never had developed them. They'd turned to brambles but he wouldn't sell. I asked him what he planned to do with that property and he said, 'Nothing.' When I asked him why, he said, 'Cause there's a wild child in there.' I didn't know what he meant. He told me a son of his had crawled into those woods soon after he was born and never was found. They could hear him late at night, though, howling with the wolves. And the old man wouldn't sell—wanted to protect his son."

Tracing grids, preparing to add the numbers. He remembers Deidre, at the age of two, trying to unfold a slip of paper. Until she had actually opened it, she didn't know what the flat piece of paper would look like, though she had watched Adams fold it seconds earlier. Now that his divorce is final, Adams sees himself in this same blank relation to Pamela and the kids.

I've made a decision, Pamela tells him (by way of asking for a loan). After long years of fast food and automobile air conditioning, of learning to ignore, for the sake of my children's uninterrupted happiness, the rapid decline of our dear urban centers, the dyeing of our air, dark, darker, as though it were an egg on Easter Sunday, the division of men into segments, the left hand literally not knowing what the right etc. (the inevitable result of a division of labor), the thinning of our bones in disgust as we bat the badminton birdie over poisonous lawns and gardens, entire communities smelling like burnt toast, the murderous revolt of our own tissue cramped as it is by carcinogens and Coke, perfume and smoke, and finally, Sam, after the failure of love, I have decided to wrap myself (along with hundreds of other women who have been running to keep the planet from crumbling under their slippered feet) around a nine-mile stretch of chain fence at Greenham Common, England, to pester and molest the young American men there dressed as soldiers, to goad them to distraction so that the deployment of medium-range American missiles cannot be accomplished with any degree of businesslike efficiency and pleasure. Joyously we will cling to one another in the mud and rain, tampons held proudly between our legs, hearts beating proudly beneath our breasts, our powerful female bodies blocking the birth of twilight. Don't try to follow me, old friend, men have been banned from the Common, a source of consternation to those of us who feel that disarmament is not specifically a feminist issue; on the other hand, those *are* men's missiles, vast and raw as Easter Island penises, leaning heavily on the children of the Soviet Union, the children of East Germany, the children of China, while their missiles lean in turn on the children of Europe, the children of the United States. Their children, our children.

Part Five

A BRIEF unexpurgated history of the world (when Toby was four years old and Adams asked him what he did today in preschool):

"We put clothes on our clothes for finger-painting and then we painted with our fingers and I ran out of paper and we took the clothes off our clothes and Mrs. Thompson she's a girl took me to the back and helped me take my clothes off so I could wet the toilet and then it was time to rest. Then we ate bananas and looked at pictures and rested some more and Mrs. Thompson took Lisa Griffin she's a girl too to the back and helped her take her clothes off so she could wet the toilet and then we rested some more when we were all dressed."

Hundreds of women. Bobbies in blue. The women dragged off by the bobbies to jail. At night the women in jail. The bobbies as husbands at home, as fathers at home with their wives. No plan, not really, not really a plan to speak of. Missiles. Gleaming white silos, a chain-link fence that runs nine miles. In the daytime mud and rain, plastic hats, the husbands as bobbies at home. Fathers of a chain-link fence. Hundreds of women in the daytime, muddy and wet, weighty, resisting the bobbies, heavy yellow plastic trying to stop the deployment of missiles. I have to go there, Pamela said, where for nine miles the world is coming to an end.

"Attending one cause to the neglect of others inevitably foreshortens knowledge of the overall effect," Adams writes in a letter to his brother. Pamela's in London. He gave her five hundred dollars to help pay for her ticket. "The right breast is just as marvelous as the left and that, in part, explains this woman's terrible arrogance."

"Carter was furious this morning," Jill tells him at dinner. "The county informed Palmer that the dam site is privately owned."

"They've changed their tune, then. I thought the county claimed that land."

"Within a week of the ground-breaking, city council dropped all legal proceedings."

"Why would they do that?"

"It's illegal for the government to fund projects on private property. The county obviously wanted to block construction of the dam."

The *Observer* carries a full account: the dam had never been intended for flood control. It was meant, instead, to be a power source, generating hydroelectricity for homes in northern Elgin County—the lots that Carter had recently sold. The dam, privately owned by Carter and a few partners (Congressman Palmer among them, Adams figures), threatened to eat into the revenues of the Elgin Utility Company.

For several days, Carter maintains publicly that he *had* planned the dam to prevent high water. When meteorologists point out that there is no such danger, Carter publishes Adams' map, with the altered isohyet. "Flash floods are an imminent possibility," he says. "We're fortunate there have been no disasters so far."

Palmer flies back from Washington for a news conference. "My record and my conscience are clear," he tells the press.

Adams fears an indictment for falsifying documents. Jill feeds him Pepto-Bismol, Nyquil, Excedrin.

Pamela has lost eight pounds. Her right elbow is cracked. She won't say much about her ten days in England (though she does give Adams her receipts): mud and rain, a few arrests. She wasn't among those taken to jail. "Dissent's the hardest thing I've ever tried to do," she says. She seems discouraged, a bit shaken.

She's been playing tricks on the children. She bought a smoke alarm, Toby says, and the other night around two it went off. He hustled Deidre out of bed and they ran into the hall. There was Pamela on a chair, pressing a button on the alarm, making it buzz. She smiled at the kids, walked into her bedroom, and shut the door.

"Maybe she was just testing it," Adams says.

"In the middle of the night?"

That's not all, Toby tells him. The day she got home she asked him to heat some roast beef for her in the microwave. He opened the oven door and was startled to see a shiny face. He dropped the roast beef on the floor. She had placed a clown mask—part of the costume she had bought months ago to tease Deidre—upright in the oven. She stood in the kitchen doorway, smiling, as Toby picked up the meat.

Near the cemetery in the least lit end of town fireflies signal their names. Again. No one dead bothers him and he doesn't think past the overhead hum of the wires.

Night is a flat color through which he's stared at his country. In quiet times, when he was a kid, he poked among car scraps in junkyards on the edge of town, looking for radios that would sing to him from someplace down the highway.

In the kitchen of the dance hall down the road, an all-night cook sends flour into the air beneath a ceiling fan. Adams can just make out the dance hall door from here. He delights, imagining the arcs of dough and the sugar he could chew until it hardened like tobacco in his mouth.

The sky's insistent clouds; the cemetery trees, top-heavy, wrapped with iron to keep them from splitting; the clasp of his own ribs. He's happy about the snow that won't fall again tonight. On calm nights it's possible even to be happy about the earth, though it's packed with victims and hides its face in an accident of rock.

His children will take care of their mother. He will take care of himself. Rosa's screen door scrapes open in wind, a sound that reminds him of home.

"Sometimes, in the middle of a séance, the dead start talking all at once," Rosa says. "I can't tell one voice from another."

I used to powder my face in the morning light through serrated curtains the green and gold sheen of the mirror hush twenty bucks I says to him for the gun in that case Smith and Wesson was a pisser wasn't it I'd say so yes train tickets grilled ham and cheese colanders seed packets a copy of *The Masses* a toy rickshaw with a paper umbrella for God's sakes hush that man could drink I haven't been thirsty in what was it like being thirsty like making love to yourself and stopping before you were through I regret to inform you opening day Ebbets Field my heart soared like a pigeon purple martins came we built a house for them hush now hush up but the sparrows made a nest in your friends and neighbors have nominated you for tomatoes the *Columbia Encyclopedia Robert's Rules of Order* black olives matchbook covers most sincerely crossword puzzles yellow paper I was sixty years old in what was it like being sixty years old not enough get me some more a shaken Mrs. Wilson informed her children good-bye honey I love you will you please be quiet keep frozen broke out in hives too soon can't rush fifty amperes warmest regards insert part A into part B then shhhh three dollars and fifty *vaya con Dios* did you twice at least no what was it like I don't remember hush.

Elgin County's legal staff is no match for Mallow and Vox, not to mention Palmer's Washington pals. Not only is the dam approved, it receives additional funding from the Bureau of Reclamation. All objections from the Elgin Utility Company are swept away, as are the protests of the individuals who had originally opposed the county."

"Everything in its place, hmm?" Carter says, signing a document that effectively terminates one-third of On-Line's employees. "With our operations streamlined, we'll show an even greater profit margin next year."

Under new policy, Jordan's position in the Records Office is absorbed by the clerical staff. Ever since the accounting department reported to Carter, rumors have been thick that Jordan was caught trying to embezzle two to three thousand dollars from the political action fund. Adams asks Carter about him.

"Unstable. Mayer warned me. I should've fired him long ago." If he suspects Jordan of stealing the money, he doesn't show it.

Adams stops by Jordan's office to say good-bye.

"You're going to have to find another boogeyman now, Sam. I'll be three thousand miles away."

Adams wishes him luck.

At five o'clock he stands at his office window. Jordan, carrying a small box containing articles from his desk drawer, steps onto a bus. The doors close behind him and he's gone.

Each friend is a light and you stare at your friends. The dark moves in. It never leaves. He sits here thinking of his debts.

The worst dreams come back like a series of bad decisions. Each has a face he can recognize: his father reading in a square of light, his mother smelling of milk, the rude and perfect taste of girls who circled his house in the dark: *I'll help you don't worry just think how long you've waited.*

Think of the friends who've looked to you, how often your help didn't matter. They fuck themselves up, you don't see them again. It's what you do all day.

Jill has let herself in with a copy of Adams' house key. Adams comes home carrying two sacks of groceries.

"Stay out of the kitchen," he tells her. "Le Grand Diner coming up."

He boils rice, bakes chicken, steams clams, mussels, peppers, tosses salad, mixes a spicy oil and vinegar dressing, butters a baguette. He sets the table with cloth napkins, lights two red candles, pours champagne. "I've been given an international assignment," he tells her.

Jill nods. "I knew it was a matter of time." She helps him carry the plates to the table. "Where?"

"Svalbard. Near Greenland." Adams passes her the salad.

"What are you doing there?"

"Carter made a deal with Comtex for exploratory mapping. They think there are undiscovered oil deposits on the island."

"How long?"

"Six months."

"Whew." She lowers her glass. "Can I visit?"

Adams smiles. "Four weeks after I get there, the sea becomes too icy for ships to navigate, and there are no commercial flights."

"Well, you know, your papers will have to pass my desk," Jill says.

Adams pours them each a glass of Amaretto. They retire to the bedroom, undress each other slowly in the reflected light from the window, and sit together on the bed.

Jill tells him of her plans: she believes she will leave On-Line within the next few months. A better offer has come her way from the physics department of Murray State College. The university's personnel director seems to have taken a romantic interest in her.

"Do you like him," Adams asks.

"I don't know." She traces a line on Adams' thigh. "Maybe."

"Then I think you should go out with him."

"I might," she says. She sips her Amaretto. A sweetened kiss.

He must renew his passport, contact the utilities, visit his parents, make arrangements for a replacement with the band. (Zig has written a song about him called Sanitized Terminal Man, "about this real straight dude who likes to get down at night.") He'd forgotten what it meant to say good-bye.

Rosa puts him in touch with his paternal grandfather, who if living would've been a hundred and thirty-two years old.

"What's it like being dead," Adams asks.

"It's like not being able to read." The voice is cold. "Imagine a grown man with no education trying to figure out his income tax or a newspaper headline or the warning label on a can of pesticide. That's death."

Adams says, "What can't you do?"

"It's not so bad, not so bad. We have our share of erotic moments, though don't ask me how. I think, somehow, we're more purely erotic without our bodies, as if the soul or energy that animated our arms and legs were not spirit or chemical reaction or electricity, but desire. But I don't know. You'd have to ask one of the others. Some of these guys seem to know what's going on here. I don't. You know what I miss? Eyes. I never realized how important eyes are."

Rosa opens her eyes and his grandfather is gone. Adams gazes out the door. Tombstones, lighted houses. Children making food with the mud beneath a tree.

His mother airs a bedroom for him. She is stooped and dark. A searing headache. "Hand me my pills," she says, folding a wet cloth on her forehead.

"How's Dad?"

"You'll see the old coot tomorrow. I invited him over for supper."

"Good. Can I get you anything else?"

"No."

"Then I'll see you in the morning."

"Good night, son."

Adams sets his glass of water on a nightstand by the bed. The moon is full. He is reminded of a night long ago. In the afternoon his mother had taken him shopping. On the way home he saw in the window of an antique store a set of toy musketeers hand-carved by a London cobbler in 1836: a toothpick army dressed in red tunics, black caps, and white belts, with brown ammunition bags on their backs. Some stood, aiming rifles. Others knelt. Still others manned tiny wooden cannons. Adams' mother let him stand in front of the window while she ran to the jewelry store down the block.

Adams pressed his fingers to the glass, pretending

to thump the wounded soldiers. Then he noticed, next to the little brigade, a display of nautical equipment: a brass telescope, a pocket watch made of gold, a silver gyroscope, and an old-fashioned rod wound tight with string. Lying open next to the rod was a captain's log bound in leather. The ink had faded to the color of a sparrow's wing. Adams couldn't read the words but he made out the date, 1798, in the upper right-hand corner of the page. Next to the log, another wonder: the captain's survey kit. Inside, encased in blue velvet folds, a wooden straight-backed compass, a ruling pin, and a divider. The instruments gleamed, their edges precise. Adams knelt closer to the glass.

Just then the shopkeeper appeared. He wore a gray suit and a tie as red as the wooden soldier's coats. He placed his right hand on a gold-leaf globe the size of a small freezer on the floor next to him, and his left hand on a Louis Quatorze chair. He scowled at Adams—he'd smudged the window. Adams turned and ran. He received a scolding from his mother, who'd searched for him for half an hour, but it didn't matter. That night, curling up in his sheets, he felt himself wrapped in velvet, the moon gleaming between the folds.

His father heats bread and thick potatoes. His face above the boiling water's light stands out, stung by the hot Nebraska air. Without words he tells Adams, "You descend from a man without foresight and are handicapped by the need to go on."

The bales behind his house are cut and carelessly stacked. Throughout the morning, combines graze on the fields; they are willful, with solid arms. Adams thinks, "This is my father's home, a scraped rock. People cry in the middle of the day and I don't know what to do with them."

Last night dust poured through the air vents like salt. A jug of fresh water waited to dry on the kitchen table. Adams cleaned the things he'd kept and went to see the river fish stirring up mud.

Okra, creamed corn, cauliflower, fried chicken, and rice. Tumblers of iced tea. Adams' father is quiet. His mother chatters about her church friends, passes biscuits and salad, asks about his upcoming trip.

After supper, Adams' father says to him, "Let's go for a spin."

They get in his pickup, an old black Ford, and drive to the miniature golf course. A Monday night, it's closed. Adams' father unlocks the gate and they stroll the carpeted greens. Windmills, castles, and moats flank the fairways under sodium vapor lights. As they walk, Adams' father knocks a blue ball ahead of them with a putter.

On all sides of the course, cornstalks scrape one another. Diesels moan on the highway.

"So you let your wife get away from you?" Adams' father says.

"Looks that way."

"Man ought not to let his wife get away from him."

"Not if it's not for the best," Adams says.

"What's that mean?" The old man sends the ball past a Plexiglas squirrel.

"What about you two," Adams asks.

"That's a different situation."

"How?"

"We'da killed each other."

A large metal buffalo blocks their path. They step around it.

"How you gonna get her back?"

"I'm not," Adams answers. "She filed for divorce. I agreed to it."

"Hell, boy." Adams' father swipes at a weed growing through a crack in the carpet. "That's bad business."

Adams watches the weed sail over the head of a mermaid curled alluringly on the edge of the thirteenth green.

"It ain't an easy path, Lord knows, but a man ought to be able to hang on to his women."

The blue ball swings around the mermaid's fin and into the cup.

"You're right," Adams says.

He phones Kenny, then Otto.

"You're going to freeze your ass off, boy."

"Probably. Listen, do me a favor and check on Pam

and the kids while I'm gone, all right? Just give them a call."

"If Pammy'll talk to me. She's a good girl, but she listens to her father."

"*Make* her talk to you. Don't let her treat you that way."

"Pammy does what she wants. You know that by now. But I'll try."

"Thanks, Otto."

"Keep a hot potato in your pants. You'll need it."

On the computer Adams simulates world climate, concentrating specifically on the northern hemisphere. He types in a climate model developed by North, Short, and Mengel of the Goddard Space Flight Center, calls a world map to the screen, and averages temperatures for the month of July over a period of a hundred and fifteen thousand years. A hundred and fifty thousand years ago glaciation covered North America and most of Eurasia. If the temperature at high northern latitudes remains below zero degrees Celsius in the summer months, ice builds slowly over decades. Presently, July temperatures fall below freezing only in Greenland and Antarctica.

Otto is right about his ass.

In the company's small library next to the coffee room he reads about a man named Milankovitch, a Yugoslav astronomer who insisted, early in the twentieth century, that the glaciation of eighteen thousand years ago (earth's most recent ice age) was caused by a small variation along the earth's axis and in the shape of the earth's orbit around the sun.

Using Milankovitch's figures as well as more recent data, Adams predicts that continental ice sheets have an oscillation period, based on earth's orbit, of roughly a hundred thousand years. He projects on the screen a simulation of continental drift and discovers that Antarctica iced over about thirty thousand years ago, after it had separated from South America and was isolated from warm equatorial waters.

Presently there is less ice on the earth's surface than there has been at any time in the past hundred and twenty thousand years. Though he knows it makes no difference in his travels, Adams is somewhat comforted by the fact.

The kids want to go for a walk in the park that Pamela takes them to, where the zoo is, and the public golf course. Adams anticipates a dreadful day, explaining what little he knows about lions, as he did when the kids were small, but the zoo is not on their list. They just want to walk.

It is a cool spring afternoon. The park is fresh, wet pines snapping under a whitecap of mist. On still days deer sometimes skip across the fairways—briefly, always a surprise—and disappear into the pines. Beyond the trees, wheat and corn sway dryly in tight little rows.

"Will you bring us something, Daddy?" Deidre says. "From that place you're going to?"

"Of course I will."

Toby, predictably, is quiet.

A V of grackles swings from the sky. Adams pulls his sweater tight around his chest. The black birds work their beaks into a collective sound like air leaking from a hose, and settle on the golf course several yards ahead. A field of black poppies, wings lifting like petals before growing still. Adams can feel his children's bodies—first Toby's, then Deidre's—break from his hands as the children rush toward the birds, flapping their arms. The grackles rise at once, gyre toward the trees, circle up, then right, descending again toward the kids, then wheel over Adams' head and are gone. Strings of mist break from the trees where the birds have made a hole, the children, meanwhile, laughing.

Part Six

WORDS for the sea:

swānrāde
brimes
yðe
wægholm
sund
eoletes

In Old English the sea is called "swan road" or "whale road," the pouting or billowy track. A ship is called a wave-traverser (yðlida) or simply sea-wood.

A flight to London, a journey by car to northern England, past Penrith and Glassonby, then into the country where Adams visits Long Meg and her Daughters, a set of ancient stones in an uneven field of gravel and broom. Legends say that Long Meg, the largest rock, was a witch, and the surrounding fragments her coven. In the days of the Celts, the witches met on this spot until Michael Scot, a Scottish wizard, turned them into stone. If the rocks are chipped or scratched, it is said, they bleed. Adams approaches Long Meg. He can smell the salt in the air, the powerful scent of the broom. Dust-spots fly off the rock and shower his coat in the breeze. He cannot imagine stones—any stone, not even a stone at the bottom of the sea—moving. Surely they drop from the sky and remain where their great weight has placed them.

North from England. In late summer Svalbard is effectively cut off from the rest of the world. The North Atlantic freezes over in winds forecasting autumn, lean chunks of ice imperil ships, commercial air flights are canceled. Only Braathen's SAFE lands on Spitsbergen, the largest island of the Svalbard group, on a permafrost landing strip in Adventdalen, the largest outpost. Comtex, however, has made its own arrangements. In Edinburgh, along with a small crew of geologists and engineers, Adams boards a four-hundred-ton, one-hundred-and-fifty-foot square-rigger named *Desire Provoked* after a point in Hudson Bay.

A shark's tail hangs from the jibboom, a voluptuous wooden maiden leads the ship into the cold Atlantic spray.

Adams stores his pack in a small cabin belowdeck. The hull is new—freshly painted metal. The cabin smells of varnish. Wooden bunk, blanket, and a quilt. A small hand mirror fastened to the wall.

One of the crew members gives the scientists a tour belowdecks. "We've recently renovated the entire ship," he says. "It was originally built in England around the turn of the century and traded mainly in sugar, rum, and mahogany. Then a Swedish exporting firm bought it, reduced it to a barkentine, and put an engine in. After the Second World War, it kicked around the Mediterranean for a while before winding up in a Greek scrapyard. Then, in '79, Comtex purchased and restored it."

He shows them the galley, the heads, and the engine room. Oil and steam. Standing water. Fresh paint. Already Adams feels cold.

The sixteenth century saw the first sea charts printed on paper. On board *Desire Provoked*, Adams discovers that paper doesn't work at sea. Documents he has packed soon become soft and moist. On deck, maps shred in his hands or become so wet with spray that the ink begins to run. The crew's maps, printed on vellum, still tear. The pilot depends for the most part on the compass and electronic equipment.

In his bunk, jostled softly against the hull, Adams realizes he's never known the past. He knows its maps, but they're only paper, bound in books or displayed in museums. The seamen's actual charts must have been destroyed at sea or reduced to illegibility. Maps printed for the public were based on explorers' notes, or on hearsay. The most accurate information was lost.

In this sense the past has broken free, like ice from a glacier, making its way over distance.

In all there are twenty-three scientists aboard *Desire Provoked*: eleven geologists, eight engineers, one landman, two marine biologists, and Adams. He has touched base with only a handful of his colleagues. The geologists he likes—they're openly curious about their surroundings. Engineers he finds aloof. An exception is Than Nguyen, a drilling engineer from South Vietnam on his first international assignment. Adams enjoys filling him in on the do's and don't's of fieldwork.

The only other person who especially interests him is a young geologist named Carol Richardson, a recent graduate of the University of Texas. As the only woman aboard, she receives much attention from her colleagues and it's hard to get a private moment with her.

After dinner one evening, Adams finds her alone on deck. She is striking, Candice Bergen with dark hair. Eyes that seem to wander on their own to the sides of her face, slightly out of focus. This has an unsettling effect, but the tension in her brow, when she concentrates and brings her vision back into line, is disarming. She appears angry and confused, then her face relaxes, her forehead pale and even. She stands at a distance from Adams, arms withdrawn, defensive.

"Do you have a cigarette?"

"No, I'm sorry, I don't smoke," Adams says.

"I quit two years ago, but I've wanted one ever since coming aboard."

"Nervous?"

"Fidgety. The cabins are so small. I'm used to lots of space—spreading my stuff out all over the place. You're the cartographer?"

"Yes."

"I have a terrible memory for faces, but I remember you from the briefing." She points to her eyes. "Plus I can't wear glasses out here. The spray."

"Ever been north?"

"Never strayed far from Texas. Until now."

"I was in Alaska in the summer of '67. People on Svalbard consider that the tropics."

Carol laughs. "I'm intrigued by what I've read of the island. I must say I never bargained for work like this."

"More comfortable in an office?"

"I figured I'd go into academics, like the rest of my family."

"What changed your mind?"

"No money in thought. Besides, when it comes to hiring, colleges are even more sexist than the private sector. It's the tenure system. Bunch of cavemen in the department at UT."

He wonders if in her view he's a caveman, wrapped tightly in his parka, trying to imagine her without a heavy coat. She smiles. They talk for a few minutes more before, chilled by a sudden squall, walking down the stairs of the companionway together.

A cat's mewling wakes Adams in the middle of the night. The sea is calm. He gets up, pulls on his pants, carefully makes his way down the narrow metal walkway between quarters in the hold. The officers are asleep. He climbs the metal stairs. No movement on deck. The canvas sails whip like towels in the wind. Adams' throat is dry. He licks his lips, swallows. Salt in his nose, his mouth. His body is being reduced to its essentials.

He stands beneath the mizzenmast, listening to the sea. Two sailors on watch smoke cigarettes in the curve of the bow. Adams is learning the ship: bowsprit, foc'sle, foremast. Poop deck at the rear. The guests' quarters are located in the hold, below the pumps.

At night, when a gale rises unexpectedly, Adams hears the cry "Aloft and stow!" The canvas, trapping too much wind, must be bound with gaskets; if not, the highest sails would blow away.

Tonight all is quiet except for the cat sounds. Adams returns down the companionway, pauses by the galley. Pots and pans rattle, but don't account for the noise. Pumps hiss, otherwise the hold is silent. He returns to his cabin, lights the kerosene lamp beside his bunk, picks up *The Travels of Amerigo Vespucci*, and reads.

. . .

Ancient visions of the other world (prior to Dante's cosmography) depicted the mysterious regions as an island or a group of islands reached by crossing a water barrier. In these accounts the ocean often is dense with swords.

The only image of the Underworld Adams remembers from college is the punishment of Tantalus: Having angered the gods, he was placed in cool water up to his neck. Luscious grapes hung above his head. When he bent to drink, the water turned to dust. When he stretched his tongue for the grapes, they rose out of reach. Perhaps spatial expressions such as "over my head" and "I've had it up to here" spring from this. "Underworld" itself is a spatial expression, remarkably resonant even today. Ways of seeing, understanding. He remembers, as a child, questioning his ability to *see*. "Can't you see I've got a headache?" his mother said. He asked her what the headaches did. "They make the whole world red." He didn't *see* until the afternoon he noticed a melted red candle on the kitchen table. Wax had dripped down the golden stem of the holder onto the tabletop glass. He imagined a candle burning inside his mother's head.

One afternoon, playing in back of the house, Adams heard a sputtering in the sky, getting louder. A small airplane came into view just above the tree line, climbed, then fell again, close to the ground. Adams ran inside to tell his mother. She was lying in the bedroom with the blinds drawn, a cool rag over her eyes. She told him to hush, she had a splitting migraine. He rushed to the window, parted the blinds. "There's nothing out there," she told him. "Now leave the blinds alone."

The plane rolled wildly out of control, trailing a plume of smoke. Adams ran outside and watched from the back porch as it dipped, its right wing just missing the water tower at the end of the block. There was a flash of light, a scattering of wood in the air. Adams ran down the block past a gathering crowd. The plane had come apart above the neighborhood and was lying out of sight. A gaping hole in the roof of a nearby house. Adams shoved his way past spectators at the front door, followed a group of men to the bathroom. Lying in the tub, a man in a crumpled suit, arms and legs at impossible angles. A thin line of water leaked from the faucet. Washcloths covered the floor.

The man's head resembled a melted red candle.

Mama's migraine, Adams thought, then someone whisked him out of the room. "There's nothing to see, nothing to see," a man said, holding people back.

He asks his colleagues at breakfast if they happened to hear a cat in the night. They shake their heads. One young geologist says his bunk is right below the pumps. "Can't hear a thing."

"You hear lots of funny noises at sea," says Harry Schock, the senior geologist. "The jibboom creaks, sails tear, bolts rattle. It doesn't mean anything. You get used to them. You'll see."

. . .

A few nights later, after dinner, Adams strolls the deck. The breeze gets cooler each evening; the air becomes thinner.

Human beings were not made to live in this environment. Though he's glad of the assignment, sometimes he misses the quiet of his kitchen.

He wonders if the kids will forget him. For the first time since leaving the States, he hopes the trip is brief.

He'll bring them something special. A piece of the North Pole. Better yet, he'll make them a map, the way he used to do when they were small. Brick roads, waterfalls, mountains. The princess who slept on the pea, Brer Rabbit, the three little pigs.

This time he'll make a magical map of the north with mythical beings like Gog and Magog roaming the Ural Mountains, waiting to break loose and storm through Europe, eating everyone in sight. He returns to his cabin, unrolls a sheet of paper. With a grease pencil he marks the center of the page longitude seventy-five degrees, latitude fifteen degrees north, the approximate location of *Desire Provoked.*

In swirling script at the bottom of the page he warns that vipers inhabit the sea: "Sailor Beware: They Will Shake a Ship to its Rafters Like a Happy Child Dancing in His Bones."

Carol says, "My father used to take the family on vacations through Texas and New Mexico. He'd point out the geological features: 'Mount Capulin, that's a volcano. See how the land here is flat and smooth? Lava has evened it out.' Or, 'This is the Permian Basin—it used to be under water.' His explanations were far more interesting than the places we stayed."

Adams nods. They've taken roast beef from the galley and climbed up on deck with it. Already the air has chilled the meat.

"I guess what he taught me," Carol says, "is that knowing how something works doesn't diminish its beauty. From a distance a mountain is gorgeous, right, then you get up close and it's just a bunch of rocks. But then if you *look* at the rocks, the mountain seems more amazing than ever. The way the mica shines or the sulfur rubs off on your hands."

"I just like to know where everything is," Adams says. "In case I need it." Carol laughs. "I remember seeing a book in the library as a child. I never read it, but the title stayed with me. It was called *You Must Know Everything*."

"Exactly," Carol says, balancing her plate on the ship's copper rail. "That's how I felt, growing up. And I love what I'm doing now, but sometimes I wonder if I'd followed other options. . . ."

"It's good that you wonder."

She smiles. Adams feels attractive.

"Well, I can't change it," she says, inadvertently brushing his sleeve. "There are lots of things—and lots of people—I'd like to get to know."

. . .

On his map for the kids Adams draws an Island of Beautiful Women.

Than invites Adams to his cabin. It's amazing what he's done with the space. Books stacked neatly in corners. Photographs of his family. An old Vietnamese flag taped to the wall. The flag is gold, with three thin red stripes running parallel through the center. Circular stains, as though someone had set a can of varnish on it, appear in one of the corners.

Than was trained at UCLA. His family remained in Saigon until the end of the war, he says, when they escaped with the last Americans.

"What was Saigon like at the end," Adams asks.

"For a long time it *wasn't* Saigon. It was a French city—like paintings of Paris, you know? Wide boulevards in the center of town, security apartments for the French civil servants. My father said a French laborer could earn more money in Saigon than a Vietnamese merchant. In school the courses we took were based on the classical French tradition. Languages and literature." He laughs. "My family complained I was getting an elitist education that wouldn't help me in my own country. When Ho Chi Minh ran the French out of the northern provinces, my father, who was not a Communist, cheered.

"Anyway, Saigon became an American city, very flashy and noisy. Money changing hands. The army tried to clean it up so it would look prosperous and democratic on the news. The cameras never showed the edge of the city where American products were dumped."

"I remember wondering before they changed the city's name if I was going to have to take Saigon off the map."

Than nods. He lights a kerosene lamp, offers Adams a cup of tea. "The first thing the American military did was to lay a new set of coordinates on the country, ignoring the old boundaries. Aggression is not always physical." He sits on his bunk. "Sometimes it takes place in the imagination. The West forced values on Vietnam that had no place in its culture. For example, here you divide the mind into conscious and unconscious. All very rational. In the East it's generally believed that the mind is unknowable, that its processes are more intuitive than rational."

"How did you get interested in science?"

"Naturally, many of us *do* value rational thought."

"Knowledge is comforting," Adams says.

Than agrees. "But on the most basic issues, I think education fails."

From A.D. 300 to 500 pilgrimages were the fashion in western Europe, from Britain to the Orient and points in between. They were not scientists, these solitary travelers on their way to the Holy Land. The first geographical documents in Europe, however, grew out of these pilgrimages. Early records are scanty, but they do mention a Gallic matron who in A.D. 31 walked across Europe to the Holy Land and returned with a shell filled with the blood of John the Baptist, murdered that year by Herod Antipas.

The first authentic guidebook dates from A.D. 330: the *Itinerary from Bourdeaux to Jerusalem*, a route to the Holy Land via southern Europe. Though mapless, it mentions cities and towns along the way, with listings of hotels and inns. The unknown author traveled on donkeys and records that the distance from Bourdeaux to Constantinople is 2,221 miles, with 112 stops and 230 changes of animals.

There are no cats aboard *Desire Provoked*, yet Adams is awakened by a whine. He's hot and muggy under the covers. The ship rocks. His left hand, limp with sleep, thumps the metal wall above his head. He listens. Again, as though the hull were being sheared.

Is there a psychological trigger for these sounds? Does the fact that he misses Toby and Deidre, for example, have a bearing on what he hears, the way latitude affects the location of a city on a map? A reasonable explanation, but the kids never had cats, unless you count the stray. . . .

The hold is quiet. He lies awake for a while, remembering the children's faces, then turns to the wall and sleeps.

From the deck of *Desire Provoked* Adams spots the first piece of ice in the sea. A small fragment, about the size of a Victorian chest of drawers.

He shivers. Long johns, two cotton shirts, a pull-over sweater, a jacket, a parka, and still he is cold. Fog hits the sails, spreading them like a bellows. They are the color of biscuits. He hunkers down against the bow. He has been reading accounts of Arctic explorers. Pytheas from Massilia—a contemporary of Aristotle's—wrote that six days north of Ireland was an island named Thule, near the frozen sea. From there northward, he reported, there was no longer a distinction between earth, air, and sea, but a strange combination of all three, a gelatinous suspension similar to a jellyfish, which made navigation, not to mention human life, impossible.

Carol taps on his door, offers him a cup of coffee. He invites her to have a seat on his bunk, lights the kerosene lamp. She picks through the sketches he has made for his kids.

"Let me show you," he says. He's fashioned a square mat of old palm fronds found in the ship's storage room. Placing his fingers on the edge of the mat, he wiggles the yellow fronds. They appear to ripple. "A living map," he says. "Wave movement." He drops tiny seashells onto the mat. "These are the islands."

"It's wonderful," Carol says. "And these?"

"Sketches for another map—a mythical guide to the north."

"They're delightful. Do you mind?" She goes through the stack. Watching her long fingers shuffle paper reminds Adams of von Frisch's famous experiments with honeybees in 1954. The scouts would locate a pollen source and then report, dancing, to the hive. The shape of the dance indicated the distance of the pollen source from the hive. A circular dance meant "nearby," a tail-wagging dance meant "far."

Adams is oddly touched that bees should have a spatial sense. Carol's dancing fingers are oddly touching, too. He sits nearer, brushing her hip.

The ocean at night breaks white and black. On deck a forgotten coat, stiff with salt, raises an arm to him as he approaches the bow. He's far from the flat country that made him—far from himself in sleepless longing for his kids. He must want to stand here tonight, turning colder with each new rush of spray.

The rigging thunders with the sails like horses rocking in their stalls. He must want to hear this. He remembers accompanying his father to a neighbor's ranch when he was ten or eleven years old. Cowboys, drunk, hugging each other, a mare who bit herself in the back giving birth. Sometimes he watched the neighbors' wives haul baskets of laundry out under the webworms' silk. The women cracked pecans in the grass and strung their clothes between the trees. Peaches barely made it through each burning spring; his father washed *his* father with a sponge.

Tonight it's all one sound: water and wind, memory and breath. He would like to say some of this to Carol

Richardson. Because of his desire for her. He would like to tell her about intimacy and maps, the direction of the hands: *He's put the old man to bed now, Carol. His father's whiskers float in a bowl of water and he looks at me, thinking something I can't name. Outside, a foal is trying to stand.*

He pulls a practice pad from his bag, takes out his sticks, and does an extended roll. He had thought life in the cold would be slow. Instead each moment is crisp, the days divided into abrupt little scenes. He tries to imagine the island of ice. Like the ocean, it is blank, ever-changing—defined for him only in texts, where words and lines can guide his eye.

On a rotating basis, members of the crew are allowed to use the communications equipment for personal business.

"How are you, honey?"

There is a moment's delay and a slight echo of his own voice before Deidre finally answers, "I'm hungry."

"Well, tell Mommy to fix you a sandwich."

"I did already."

"Do you miss me?"

"Yes. Come home and watch me dance."

"I will soon. I love you."

Toby says "Hi."

"How's school," Adams asks.

"Fine."

"You taking care of your sister?"

"I'm trying not to bug her."

"I'm going to bring you something special."

"Great."

Pamela comes on the line. "Take care of yourself, Sam."

"I will. Anything you need?"

"A straitjacket for Toby." She laughs. "Otherwise everything's smooth."

"I'll call again as soon as I can. They don't give us much time on this thing." (Conversations must be as brief as possible, and messages must be truthful, according to the manual.)

Adams overhears Carol talking to a young man in Austin, Texas. "Remember the Willie Nelson concert when you took off your shirt?"

He wishes he knew guitar. It's hard to play Willie Nelson on a practice pad.

"Have you heard noises at night?" They are sitting on Carol's bunk.

"I sleep like a baby at sea. What kind of noises?"

"Like cats, close to the hull. But I can't locate them."

"Maybe your bunk's near a stress point." She lowers the kerosene lamp.

"Tell me about your friend in Austin."

Carol lies back on the bunk. "We lived together for

a while. His name is Jack," she says. "Neither one of us wanted to settle down, really. We agreed to see other people, he moved out."

"And?"

"I don't know." She sits up on one elbow. "I'm jealous of the women he meets. And the men I've gone out with may as well have died in a war or something. I think, sometimes, a whole generation of American men has been ruined. They say the first World War wiped out every English boy between seventeen and thirty—well, that's how it feels. Like nuns have been sending brain waves out to all the men in the country, fucking them up forever."

"What's wrong with them? Us?"

"You're always running. I swear, the business world is full of these asexual men living by the clock, putting all their energy into contracts and torts and things. I mean, careers are important and all, but there's an inordinate number of guys out there whose lives are nothing *but* careers. And I think a lot of men are turning gay because they're fucked up about women."

"You're not serious."

Carol shrugs. "*Something's* going on. They couldn't handle Women's Lib or Vietnam or *something*. American men are just wimps."

"Was Jack a wimp?"

"He couldn't make a commitment. But then neither could I, I'm not being fair. It's just that . . . my feelings are hurt." Adams rubs her neck. "I feel rejected when I want to feel enjoyed."

Adams smooths her dark hair (she is fragrant), holds his lips against her temple. "I'm over forty," he says. "I'm fucked up, but maybe in different ways than you're used to."

Carol smiles. He holds her breast. "Not so hard," she whispers. They rock with the motion of the ship. She has opened the port above her bunk and soon their hair is glistening with salt spray.

Carol's hips are narrow—he feels that he will break her. "It's okay," she says, pulling him closer against her. She wets the tip of a finger and rubs his nipple. Her touch is so light he can barely feel it, yet he is tingling in his shoulder, all the way down to his elbow, where a pool of sensation has him frozen. They are awkward with each other, out of synch. He begins to think of Pamela, Jill . . . but Carol is a surprising lover. She becomes daring, excited when he least expects it, gripping the base of his neck, pulling him down. Before they are through, she has brought him back to *her*.

He is twelve years Carol's senior, Mesozoic to her Paleozoic, Cretaceous, reptilian, seed-bearing, of relatively short duration, whereas she is Carboniferous, amphibian, seaweed and spore, full of new life testing its legs. If they grow together they will never *be* together. Her Shepherd Kings will just be setting up shop in northern Egypt while his Joan of Arc is being burned at the stake. In the night she reaches for him with affection and assurance.

Icebergs: yellow mist, yellow ocean. The wooden rigging of *Desire Provoked* looks yellow in the fog. Adams sips hot yellow tea, leans against the railing. A giant slab of ice breaks the mist, water lapping its base. To the port side another slab, then another, like one-story office buildings. Their movements are abrupt, broken by the sea. Quietly *Desire Provoked* slides past them, its sails lax and yellow.

When Adams and Carol make love, they stroke each other carefully. Their hands are rough from handling rope. Twice a day they are asked to assist the regular crew in raising and lowering sails. The ropes are smooth and white, made of polyester fibers, but burn when tugged through the hand. Gloves don't help much. To keep the ropes from chafing, the crew has wrapped them in pieces of leather or split pieces of garden hose.

Adams has learned the eight essential knots that every seaman needs: the figure eight, the square knot, the sheet bend, the bowline, the clove hitch, the double-half hitch, the fisherman's hitch, and the rolling hitch. In the evenings, when the wind is steady, Adams' task is to tie the jib sheets to the clew, accelerating ship's speed. Adams gazes at the sails. They are beautiful white surfaces, curved with the wind. He remembers

Deidre sticking her arm out the car window (a habit he tried to break). When she held her palm flat, her arm was forced straight back, but when she cupped her hand, she felt less stress. *Desire Provoked*'s sails work on the same principle. He imagines maps painted on the canvas, vivid colors pointing home.

"Magnetic north is located at about seventy-six degrees north, a hundred and one degrees west," the helmsman explains. "It's not the same as true north, which lies almost directly beneath the polestar, so we've got to make adjustments. I prefer old-fashioned potato navigation myself. You toss the potatoes ahead of the ship as you go. When you don't hear a splash, you turn the son-of-a-bitch *fast*."

One of the engineers manages to collect small sections of an iceberg as *Desire Provoked*, in still waters, floats by. Adams takes a piece about the size of a golf ball, and with bright red colors draws on it the petals of a flower. After supper he presents it to Carol. She holds it in her palm, and slowly they watch the flower melt.

In 1613 William Baffin piloted one of seven ships fitted out by the Muscovy Trading Company, and traveled to Spitsbergen to fish and whale.

From Baffin's journal: "Upon this land there be manie white beares, graie foxes, and great plentie of deare; and also white partridges, and great store of white fowle, wilde geese, sea pigeons . . . and divers others, whereof some are unworthy of naming as tasteing. The land also doth yield much drift wood, whales finnes . . . and some times unicorn hornes."

Adams sets the journal down. He shivers, lights the kerosene lamp, pulls on his parka. He can smell his breath. Fumes from the lamp warm his throat.

He picks up the journal again: "Theise things the sea casteth forth upon the shoare, to supplie unreasonable creatures on the fruitless land, the country being altogether destitute of necessaries wherewithal a man might be preserved in time of winter."

Something's tearing the hull. He gets up, explores the hold, but cannot locate the noise. It seems general, throughout the area belowdecks. The following morning, when he reports to the ship's skipper, he's given the standard line: "You'll get used to the noises at sea."

"Here is a book you might enjoy," Than tells Adams. They are sitting in Than's cabin, sipping tea.

Adams picks up the book. *The Philosophy of Hegel.* He thinks of Jurgen and laughs. "Why?" he says.

"For Hegel, Reason is the generating principle of the universe. A philosophy compatible with your thoughts."

"Maybe." Adams smiles.

"In Vietnam men sometimes hold hands in public—

it's part of friendship, an accepted custom. Americans can never get used to that. It unsettles them. This book." He taps Hegel. "Affected me the same way. My introduction to the West."

Adams laughs. "If you're going to practice science here, Than, you'll have to adopt a Western bias. You'll have to trust objective methods."

"I do. But there are problems with that."

"Like what?"

He thinks for a moment. "Let's say that you and I are walking down a street and we see—what? A television antenna on a building, all right? How tall is it? From a distance of two kilometers it appears to have one height. If we move closer, it appears to be taller."

"So we measure it."

"With a notched tape, standing next to it. Is that an accurate measure?"

"I see what you're saying," Adams interrupts. "What gives the tape authority?"

"Exactly. Our standards are someone's invention. How tall is the antenna? One meter. What is one meter? The length of this tape. What is the length of this tape? The height of the antenna."

"But we agree on the standards."

"Still, they exclude a wide range of perceptions. We know our own knowing, that's all. *Interpretation* is all we have."

Adams shakes his head. "I interpret from the growling in my stomach that I'd rather eat than talk."

Than laughs. "It's getting late, isn't it?"

They rise. "There's something about the fog and the cold," Adams says. "Turns you inward."

"Where you find the center."

Sea stories: after supper several members of the crew leave the galley, walk up the companionway stairs, and stand on the poop deck, smoking. "Sailing alone does funny things to a man," says one. "I tried it once. Eight days out to sea, I heard voices saying, 'Go back to land.' "

"You know the story of Joshua Slocum, don't you?"

The crewmen nod.

"We don't," Carol says.

"Slocum was a down-and-out sail captain, couldn't find no work 'cause the steamer's so popular. He sets out on an old oyster sloop named *Spray*, aimin' to be the first man to sail around the world by himself."

"He done it, too," says the first speaker.

"Yeah, but three days out to sea he got the cramps. He'd been eatin' plums and cheese. So he goes below, sits there sick at his stomach, and finally falls asleep. When he wakes up, he can feel ol' *Spray* heaving into the wind. He crawls up top and there's an old man with a red cap at the helm. He says he's the captain of the *Pinta* and he's come to guide the ship. Then he lays into Slocum for mixing plum with cheese. 'White cheese is never safe unless you know where it comes from,' he says. Slocum faints again, and the next day he sees he's still on course. To the end of his life he claimed what he saw was real. 'I's grateful to the old pilot,' he said, 'but I wondered why the hell he didn't take in the jib.' "

After two weeks at sea, Adams has become a meteorologist of sorts. Though the ship receives broadcasts from the United States National Weather Service, he prefers to make his own predictions. He listens to weather broadcasts on the AM band, sketches maps from day to day, noting cold fronts, warm fronts, high and low pressure systems, wind direction, and temperature changes. Using this data, combined with fog readings, Adams has learned to spot weather trends and is quite proud of himself, though the crew laughs at his enthusiasm.

He is particularly good at predicting winds. At an altitude of three thousand feet, wind direction parallels the prevailing weather system, and on the ocean the wind is two thirds the velocity of high-altitude currents.

Adams walks out on deck, says casually but confidently, "Wind's going to pick up tonight."

The sailors bundle up and laugh.

North winds send hail,
South winds bring rain;
East winds we bewail,
West winds blow amain.

After supper one evening (green beans, roast beef, banana pudding), Adams checks his charts, predicts high winds. That night he is awakened by cats screaming. Shortly afterwards, "Aloft and stow!" He is thrown violently against the hull. He tries to stand, cannot. People yelling from their quarters. Finally he makes it to the door. The crew is running in the hold, water pouring down the companionway. He cannot get his balance. The captain announces that *Desire Provoked* has hit gale force winds (isn't it the other way around, Adams wonders). Everyone is ordered to remain belowdecks until further notice. Carol crawls out of her cabin. She huddles with Adams at one end of the hold. She's sick. Adams grips her waist as she coughs and spits. Than brings her a towel from his cabin.

The storm continues through the night. The following morning, calm water. *Desire Provoked* sails limply, tattered, tilted at an angle. The compass is shattered; the Loran-C receiver is out.

The pilot tells the captain they're off course.

"How much?"

"It'll take a while to determine our position. Without the Loran it's largely guesswork. The RDF's still working—"

"We're too far out to receive signals."

Desire Provoked drifts for a day and a half. Heavy fog. On the second day an object appears on the horizon. With their instruments out, the crew cannot determine their distance from it. Adams knows that if he can figure the object's height, and his own height above water, he can calculate the range of visibility between it and him. Using a hand-held compass and a divider, he estimates the object's height.

approx. geographical range (nautical mi.)

$$1.144\sqrt{\text{object height}} = \text{range of visibility}$$

He determines the height of his eye above water, estimates his own range of visibility. Then he adds the two results to determine the approximate distance between the object and the ship. Hastily he sketches a Circle of Position chart (where every object on its circumference is equidistant from the center of the circle). With a sextant he measures vertical angles, smooths his drawing compass across the chart.

He points to a spot in the ship's atlas. "We're here. Not far from where we were."

Studying the atlas, he presumes the object to be a lighthouse on the coast of Bear Island. He thumbs through the *Light List*. The Bear Island lighthouse has a Fixed and Flashing light, red to green.

"That would explain why we've seen no light," says the captain. "In bad weather, red and green are harder to see than white."

Adams also discovers in the *Light List* that the tower contains a radio beacon. He switches on the RDF and receives a signal. *Desire Provoked* is, indeed, off the southwest coast of Bear Island, another day from Svalbard.

. . .

"Very impressive," Than says.

Adams laughs. "We agreed there's no true standard of measurement."

"In a manner of speaking. But you *did* determine our position."

"Yes."

"Logical. Practical."

"You won't mind, then, if I learn what I can?" Adams smiles.

"No, no. But be careful."

"Too much reading makes you crazy?"

Than heats a cup of tea. "In 1967, where I lived, it was impossible not to find on certain country roads American mines in the shape of dogshit. It took very clever minds to disguise the bombs, but they failed to realize that there were no dogs in the country. Napalm had driven them away, so the mines fooled no one. All that learning, technology, and effort, and it was in the end exactly what it looked like."

From the preliminary information packet Adams received on boarding *Desire Provoked*: "Svalbard belongs to the Kingdom of Norway. A governor (*sysselman*) presides over its domestic interests. In December 1975 the total population of Svalbard was 3,431: 1,177 Norwegians and 2,254 Russians, concentrated on Spitsbergen Island.

"On the west coast of Spitsbergen, the temperature rarely drops below −30 degrees centigrade, and in summer rarely exceeds +10 degrees centigrade."

Harry Schock, the senior geologist, calls a meeting of all scientists aboard ship. They gather in a tiny drawing room near the galley. "All right, listen up," he says. "Before we get to Svalbard, you need to know some things. There's a lot of tension between Norway and the Soviet Union. It started in '61 when Norway granted American Caltex Oil two hundred prospecting claims based on geological indications, maps, aerial photographs, the works. In '63 Arktikugol, a Russian oil company, applied for a claim. They had the same type of evidence, but Norway turned them down. Arktikugol filed a complaint and finally the Department of Industry granted the claim. Otherwise they'd be violating Svalbard's principle of equal treatment."

Before leaving the United States, Adams had requested through a Comtex spokesman oblique and vertical photographs of the Svalbard archipelago. He was told that the Norwegian Polar Institute, in the interests of fair play, no longer made aerial photographs available to foreign commercial interests. His job cannot begin before he sets foot on Spitsbergen.

Comtex wants him to concentrate on Svalbard's continental shelf: to explore it with the geologists and prepare contour charts. There are political problems with this, too. At times Norway opens the shelf to commercial exploitation; then, without warning or explanation, the shelf is declared off-limits.

Adams' latest information gives him the go-ahead, though he's warned that tension is high on the island.

The Norwegians feel undercompensated, and the Russians, who outnumber every other group on the island, do not welcome Comtex.

In two and a half weeks at sea, Adams has hardly had time to think of home. In private moments, working on his map, he has wondered if the kids are eating junk food, if they're getting enough sleep. Is Pamela bringing strangers home to bed? He has the sense that his responsibilities are on hold, waiting for him to return.

He sits on his bunk, unrolls the children's map, weights one corner with Hegel, and sketches the Island of Reason, surrounded by mist.

Desire Provoked is scheduled to dock at the southern tip of Spitsbergen Island. From there Adams and the others will fly inland. At the airfield, American, Norwegian, and Soviet officials closely monitor one another's activities. In addition, Soviet scientific expeditions are allowed to move freely throughout the archipelago; frequently, says Harry Schock, these expeditions are reconnaissance activities, attempts to inspect other nations' progress in exploring the islands. The Soviets make no secret of their aims, though Norway has warned that surveillance of this type violates Norwegian sovereignty. Schock tells Adams and his colleagues not to resist any such inspection by Soviet "scientists." "The best way to defuse tension," he says, "is not to create it in the first place."

. . .

Adams says good-bye to the sailing crew of *Desire Provoked*. Among the icy docks with its canvas folded, the ship looks abandoned. Before leaving the harbor, Adams learns that eighteen feet of the inner hull had been sheared by heavy equipment: his noises at night.

The scientists board a plane for Barentsburg, on the west coast. There they will undergo a briefing and be assigned specific duties.

The flight is short. Adams, Carol, and Than sit in the rear of the plane with backpacks and equipment, huddling together in their parkas. The land below is a solid white sheet of snow. *Mørkitiden*, Norwegian winter.

Barentsburg has no distinguishing features. Hard snow crackles beneath their feet once they leave the permafrost landing site. Adams can see only swirling flakes as he makes his way to a dark green wooden building resembling a barracks. Inside, the scientists are offered coffee and doughnuts, and asked to sit on metal folding chairs facing a raised platform.

"This looks like an army briefing," Carol tells Adams. He nods. Even inside the building their breath turns to smoke.

A man named Pepperstone mounts the platform, asks them to make themselves at home. "Svalbard is not particularly pleasant this time of year," he says, "but you'll become accustomed to the conditions." He is a heavy man with a blond beard. He gestures to his right. "We have a room full of beds back here, along with lavatory facilities. You'll be spending the night here, then tomorrow morning you'll be flying to specific locations along the coast to begin your work."

Arrangements have been made for Carol to sleep alone in a tiny room. The men will sleep in a large room in metal spring beds placed side by side. Carol's room is just off the kitchen and the walls are thin. Even if there was more privacy, it is too cold to make love.

Before supper, Adams shaves (the tap water stays warm for just a few seconds) and changes. He joins his colleagues in a large chilly room. Picnic tables and folding chairs have been arranged in rows. Meat loaf and peas: though the food is warm, it tastes frozen.

"I feel like I've been drafted," Carol says.

"They're very organized," Than agrees.

"I expected more of a welcome."

"It must be hard to get anything done here," Adams says. "They've got to be all business." Still, he too is a little disappointed in the barrenness of the place, the brief formality of their welcome.

After supper members of the expedition line up to call their families on radiotelephones.

"Jack has probably fallen in love with one of those women who sell turquoise bracelets on Guadalupe Street," Carol says. "I'll be a voice from his past."

Adams notes that he has not been enough to make her forget about Jack. She squeezes his hand.

When Adams finally gets a turn, he radios Pamela's

house. The kids are asleep. He'd forgotten all about the time difference. "I'm sorry if I woke you," he says.

"That's all right. So you made it okay?"

"Yes."

"What's it like?"

"Cold. Nothing but snow."

"Prettier than Alaska?"

"Nowhere near."

Waves of static. "I remember when you went to Alaska. It's exciting to get postcards from faraway places."

Adams nods, realizes she can't see him.

"We were just married. I missed you."

"I miss the kids," Adams tells her.

A long pause. "Have you met anybody interesting," Pamela asks.

"No."

"I'm meeting all sorts of interesting people through the galleries. A sculptor from San Francisco's in town this week."

"That's wonderful."

"I sold a new piece. The moon. On a coat hanger. In a closet."

"Congratulations." The line squeaks. "They're going to cut me off soon. Are the kids all right?"

"Deidre's got a dance recital next Sunday. And Toby's been pretty calm."

"Tell them I love them."

"I will."

"I have to go now."

"All right. Sam?"

"Yes?"

"They miss you, too."

Fitful sleep. The room is cold, the bed hard, the pillow too soft. For extra support he places *The Philosophy of Hegel* under his head. He lies awake listening to the wind scratch the wire-and-glass windows.

Carol's in the next room. He can't help feeling that their attachment is temporary, dependent on the circumstances, yet when the other men look at her he feels possessive.

He misses Jill.

Forty-one years old. Incredible.

He clutches his legs to his chest and tries to sleep.

The following morning the scientists are divided into groups and flown to designated points along the coast to begin exploratory work. Than is scheduled to fly to a valley forty-five miles west of Barentsburg. "See you here in a few weeks," he says.

"By then I'll have mastered Hegel."

Adams and Carol are flown to the same spot—a site near Ny-Alesund, northwest of Barentsburg. There are only a few temporary buildings—a generating plant, a fuel depot, a maintenance shop, and three plastic bubbles, geodesic domes. Behind the bubbles, two metal tunnels, like corrugated sewer pipe, large enough to shelter six horses.

"The company's too cheap to give us snowmobiles," says one of the scouting engineers. He has been here two weeks. "A horse is handy if you're traveling more'n a mile."

Carol's assigned to check a series of core samples that the drilling engineers have already collected. The men are obviously delighted to see her, and she stays close to Adams.

Adams must go up in a Cessna to take some aerial photographs. The sky is overcast, thick at intervals, and condensation forms on the windows of the cockpit. The pilot says, "That's it for now."

When they try again in the afternoon, the same conditions prevail. Adams can't see a thing out the cockpit window. A sudden change in pressure jolts the plane. Adams' stomach turns over. When the pilot lands, the craft skids several yards, spinning sideways on a sheet of ice. Adams opens the door, steps unsteadily onto the snow.

"I've had several offers already," Carol tells Adams. They are sitting inside a plastic bubble, warming themselves by a portable heater. The plastic wriggles with the wind. "These two guys hung around looking over my shoulder while I worked. I barely got anything done." She picks up a small leather bag. "They gave me some pot. I don't have the stomach for it anymore, but it's better than beer and I gotta have *something* out here. Want some?" She rolls a cigarette, lights it, inhales, and offers it to Adams. He takes it from her.

"It never did much for me," he says. "The only time I had it was in Alaska. This was '67, height of Vietnam, all that. Most of us on the field trip were just out of graduate school, thrilled to be making money. Thought we were real radicals sitting out in the middle of nowhere passing pot." He takes a short puff.

"I'll be glad when we get back to Barentsburg."

"So will I," Adams says. "I can't do a thing until the weather clears."

"Based on what I saw today, there's a good chance of activity here. Those core samples have good permeability."

Adams smiles.

"What?"

"How's *your* permeability?"

"If you don't mind a little frostbite, you can check."

"I don't mind."

"We should probably join the others for supper."

"I guess." He strokes her arm. "But don't eat too much. We've both got to squeeze into your sleeping roll."

Clear skies. Up in the Cessna, Adams snaps the terrain. The sunlight reflecting off the snow is blinding, and for a second Adams wonders if the glare, like concentrated light through a lens, might set the wings of the plane on fire.

The pilot circles the snowy rifts seven times before Adams says he has enough pictures.

Back at the camp, Carol's frying bacon and slicing cheese for lunch. She has a cut on her lip.

"What happened?" Adams says.

With the knife she points out one of the men sitting beside a Coleman stove. "He tried to kiss me. When I pulled away, he bit."

"I'll talk to him."

She flashes him an impatient look. "Eat your lunch. We don't need any macho scenes out here."

Bacon grease spatters over the pan and sizzles in the snow.

"Halloo!" someone calls.

Behind the camp, at a distance of two or three miles in the direction of the coast, there's a line of hills. Against this backdrop seven or eight men are walking toward the camp carrying backpacks. One of them raises his hand. "Halloo!" he calls again.

"Russians," says the man who kissed Carol. "They checked us out the day we got here."

To the very last man, the Russians are big, bearded, ruddy. Carol offers them coffee. The leader, a red-head, smiles, nods at Adams. "American?" he says.

"Yes."

"How do you like our island?"

"It's very cold."

The Russians laugh as if he's made a joke.

"You are here for oil?"

"I'm here to draw maps."

"Maps? I thought Norwegians gave you Americans maps?"

"The Department of Industry won't release any cartographic information."

"Ah, that's what they say." He motions to Carol for another cup of coffee. "But we hear American oil companies get whatever they want."

"You hear wrong."

Carol's eyes widen. Did he say that?

"Is that so? We are, at any rate, forced to work in the dark. In this area in particular our charts are inaccurate. We have not been able to explore the region to our satisfaction. Could you supply us with information?"

"I'm afraid I can't," Adams says. "Beyond preliminary sketches, we have nothing as yet."

The Russian spreads his arms. "You have committed all these people and you have no information?"

"We have scouting reports," Carol says, stepping close to Adams.

"As I said, preliminary information is all we have to go on. I've only been here two days. This morning was the first time the weather cleared enough for me to take accurate aerial photographs and trigonometric measurements."

The redheaded man tosses his coffee into the snow.

"Do you mind if we have a look at your preliminary information?" he says.

The Russian team rummages through backpacks, bedrolls, crates. A clatter of cooking utensils. Carol blushes when the redheaded man opens a bag containing her personal belongings. He carefully unfolds her long johns.

Satisfied, he extends his hand toward Adams. "We are working in the vicinity," he says. "I am sure that when you obtain your information, you would have no objections to sharing it with us?"

"Not at all," Adams says.

"Good."

At night he develops photographs with clumsy portable equipment. The red bulb above the fixing tray lights crystals in the diamonds of the plastic bubble. He is fortunate that the sun was low when he took the pictures. The stakes he had set out as markers are invisible in the glare, and the long shadows create relief in what would otherwise have been grainy white fields.

Meanwhile Carol studies core samples and rocks supplied by the engineers. She is encouraged by the signs. "Get me a map soon, will you?"

Tracing lines across the pictures, Adams imagines his own world sectioned off into patterns. Carol nearby, tethered to him with a tight elastic band. Carter at a very sharp angle, difficult to watch. Far off, so far he can barely see them, Pamela and the children. Their lines are slack. When he tugs, he sometimes gets a faint response.

Adams requests recent American satellite photographs of the Arctic. Three days later the pilot returns with a stack of pictures. Adams compares them with the more detailed shots he had taken earlier.

He wishes he had a gravimeter and a set of seismic probes, but must be content with metal pillows to record topographic shifts. Lead-shielded packets of Cobalt-60, emitting gamma rays, help define the terrain, as do the tellurometer (a two-way microwave system) and theodolite (a sighting tube with horizontal and vertical scales).

None of the instruments is completely reliable by itself, and Svalbard is so heavily glaciated that it is difficult to determine the island's actual topography. He must record a number of observations and test them against one another. There is no room for misinterpretation; faulty mapping could encourage drilling on a precarious site.

He produces a rough map for Carol.

"It's amazing how glaciation has smoothed out most of the terrain," she says, "but overall, the structure's what I expected. This, with the core samples, ought to be enough to lay in a claim for a drilling permit."

"Good," Adams says. "We've got to run the sound

tests on the shelf. Then we can head back to Barentsburg."

"And privacy."

At night around the fire the engineers drink beer and challenge one another to run naked into the snow. The one who goes farthest gets to sleep late the following day. Tonight there is a tie; the two men shiver near the fire and the Coleman stove, their faces blue. Adams and Carol join them for supper.

"I saw a polar bear this morning," one says. "Mile or so from the hills."

"Big?"

"You bet. Thick yellow fur . . . spooked my horse a little, but it wasn't much interested."

"Shoulda shot it. I'm getting tired of bacon."

"I don't have a license to carry a gun here."

"You know they don't let the Russians carry weapons?"

"Damn straight. I don't want those bastards poking around here with rifles."

After several more beers it is generally agreed that if the Russians return to camp, they'll get their asses kicked.

Carol is asleep. The camp is quiet. Adams lies awake inside the plastic bubble, listening to the wind whip snow around the embers of the fire, the equipment, and tents. The horses chuff and stamp. Ice breaks.

Manscathers. Walkers in the waste.

Old English words for fear.

Gog and Magog.

He wonders where the Russian camp is. Perhaps Redbeard is awake, listening to the ice.

In a geologically active world, what does territoriality mean?

Vyduv: a Russian tribal word for "wind-swept plain." The man who kissed Carol taught him that.

In two weeks on the island he has seen seven different types of snow: star, plate, needle, column, column with a cap at each end, spatial dendrite, irregular.

One day, pacing out distance on a plain, he paused by his horse to listen. The ground bristled. Worms by the thousands surfaced in a snowbank: *Mesenchytraeus*, a distant relative of the earthworm. Ladybugs, too, insulated in deeply packed drifts.

He'll take some to Carter.

He gazes through the plastic bubble at the stars. In the daytime the sky becomes a map. The sun is so intense in the thin air that it glares off the ground, making shapes on the clouds. Reading shadows in the sky, Adams can determine if there is water or rough terrain ahead. At night he's blind. Light travels so slowly through space. The star at the end of the Dipper appears to him tonight as it was when the first American colonists plotted revolution. What's up there now?

Carol turns over in her sleep. A thunderous crash along the coast: another block of ice has broken free.

. . .

From the U.S. Army manual on survival: "On exceedingly cold nights, dig a hole in the ground, place your weather balloon in the hole so that half of it rests in the snow. Cover the other half with snow a foot deep and let it set for an hour. Tunnel into the balloon, deflate it, and leave the snow dome standing free. Snow, packed tightly, provides sufficient warmth for short-term survival."

Adams was issued an Army manual at Barentsburg. But not a weather balloon.

The Russians return. Redbeard offers them a nearly frozen bottle of Scotch, looks around shamelessly, asks Adams what progress he has made.

"I know the area pretty well," Adams says.

Redbeard is discomfited. "You have numbers," he asks.

Adams shows Redbeard his map.

"You have accomplished no more than we have."

Adams pours himself a cup of Scotch.

"You expect to find oil?"

"I'm not a geologist," Adams tells him.

Redbeard turns to Carol. She says nothing.

"There is not enough oil here to make it worth your while."

"We'll see," Adams says. He passes the bottle to Redbeard, who pours himself a cup. Then, to his own astonishment, Adams begins to remove his parka. "Care to join me in a race?" he says.

Ten minutes later, naked Russians run around him in the snow. The bottle is tossed to and fro until it shatters on a sheet of ice. Adams tumbles wildly into a snowdrift—the shock stuns him for a moment. The bare-assed burly men, chests heaving, follow him with prancing steps. The hair on their legs is frozen. They point to one another's white bodies, laughing with painful abandon.

Adams loads a pack, saddles a horse with help from one of his colleagues. "I'll be back after lunch," he tells Carol. "I want to check the coast."

Forty minutes later he has reached the base of a small snowy cliff. He stops to rest. In his heavy coat he feels warm. The horse is warm. He can see no passage through the cliffs to the sea. He shoulders his pack, dismounts.

He finds a manageable spot on the face of the cliff and digs in his hands. Halfway up, the snow gives out beneath his feet. A low creaking noise. He tumbles backwards.

The slab of ice in his hands disintegrates. Fragments spin about him as he falls, glittering needles shattering in front of his face. Snow swirls into his eyes. A sudden rush of wind knocks the breath out of him.

He feels pressure on his back and legs. Ribs ache. He didn't fall too far. That probably saved his life. He is pinned, not by ice but by several feet of snow. When the temperature warms and the snow melts a bit, he'll be able to move. Nothing, he thinks, is broken except one of his bicuspids, upper right. He can wiggle it with his tongue.

Stupid, trying to climb pure snow.

His backpack lies within reach of his left hand. The horse has wandered off a few yards.

His watch shattered in the fall, but he figures someone's looking for him by now. A light snow has begun—the first in days. If it turns heavy, his tracks will be obscured.

He twitches the muscles in his legs and toes. He can still feel his extremities. The snow is getting heavier.

His tooth aches. He wiggles it, spits blood. His gum throbs—pain in the back of his neck, at the top of his head. He presses the tooth with his tongue, trying to stop the throbbing. The tooth comes loose and he spits it onto the snow.

The discomfort comes from not moving. The snow is actually warm, much warmer than the wind. He doesn't know how long it takes to get frostbite.

They won't come after him until the snow lets up.

He digs a shallow hole beneath his head, shoves the backpack in it, and rests his cheek against the cloth. He can feel the circulation in his head.

The main thing is not to struggle. Stay calm, wait for a bit of clearing. Move only enough to stay warm.

He remembers hearing that polar bears have a

nictitating membrane in their eyes, to wipe the slush away. His own eyes sting. He can barely see his hands.

For an hour or so the blizzard clears. It's warmer—the snow on his back breaks up a bit. He moves slowly, deliberately. If he overexerts, he'll start to sweat and his clothing will grow damp.

Soon the snow begins again, visibility is reduced once more. Still, he doesn't rush. Dimly, he sees his horse lie down in the snow.

Assuming the blizzard continues, what method will his colleagues use to find him? Rescue systems are well coordinated in resort areas and major scientific outposts; though Comtex has not yet made a commitment here, surely the engineers came equipped.

A device to trace his heartbeat (would it be muffled by snow?) or detect his body heat. No—the snow he upset when he fell is thick, temperature will vary wildly from mound to mound.

X-ray fluorescence? Radar?

In the seventeenth century rescuers set bowls of water on the rubble after an avalanche. In the water floated pieces of bread. Wherever the bread "pointed" the rescuers dug for victims.

The wind howls like air inside a shell.

He reaches into his backpack. A geologist's pick. *The Philosophy of Hegel*. An extra pair of drumsticks.

Whatever possessed him to pack these things? He

longs for warm sand, tropical fruit. Coconuts, bananas, berries. The cold, sharp pang of juice.

A man springs, fully clothed, from the snow where Adams spit the tooth. The tooth is gone. The man looks at Adams, picks up the backpack, walks away, pausing only to pat the freezing horse's nose.

Stop this.

He's hungry. He's hallucinating.

If he could send a new self into the world, how would he act? Take Carol home? Fight for his kids? Would he be a smarter man, stronger, more articulate than the one beneath the snow?

Both his arms are free. He can move his legs. Sore but intact. He feels the pack beneath his cheek. For some reason he thought he'd lost it.

He digs with the pick and the drumsticks—9A, thin, not much good in the snow. If only his hands were bigger. The snow is starting to harden, but he's got room to wiggle.

A half hour later he's free.

Standing unsheltered in the wind, he shivers. He tries to build a shelter of ice, but this proves ineffective. He can already feel the effects of hypothermia.

The horse lies in the snow like something dropped from the sky. Not quite dead. Adams huddles near it for its body heat, but the temperature continues to drop.

Without thinking, he lifts a heavy chunk of ice from the avalanche pile and brings it down on the horse's skull. With his pick he slices the belly, hollows out a space inside, removing the internal organs. They are slippery, bilious, gray. He is nauseated, but his stomach is empty. He takes a deep breath and crawls inside.

He can only stand lying inside the horse for a period of, he guesses, one hour. Then the smell gets to him and he has to crawl outside. His clothes are damp with snow and blood, the wind eats through him.

He sits beside the dead animal, smelling of shit, clots of hair, bone, and blood. He rubs his face, balls of hard flesh stick to his lips. He opens his mouth, the crumbs fall onto his tongue; slowly he chews. The animal creaks like an old chair whenever he lifts the stiff flap of ribs and hair, icy now, to crawl in or out.

From time to time he hears sounds. Looks around. Shouts.

He's afraid to sleep. His legs are numb. He stumbles out of the horse, walks a few steps to keep the blood moving, drinks water from a piece of ice, curls up again inside the horse.

To stay awake he thinks of Pamela and the kids. Deidre, naked in the tub; Toby, naked on the floor of his room, doing sit-ups; Pamela, naked in his arms.

Why are they all naked?

His body has grown too stiff inside the horse. He

crawls out and walks around, vigorously rubs his legs.

He can't find his tooth in the snow. It has become a man and walked back to camp. They won't come looking for him now.

The horse's body is losing its heat. Soon it will be a rock, frozen.

His cheek stings. He has fallen asleep on the ice. No snow. No wind. A rapidly clearing night sky. He pulls himself up, grabs his pack. He pauses, wondering what to do with the horse.

He doesn't have the strength.

His lips are chapped. He licks them, feels a gap in his gum. Did he lose a tooth?

His muscles relax as he walks. Feeling returns to his feet and hands.

He imagines Carol, or tries to. He cannot picture her. He has forgotten what she looks like. Without touching his face he tries to recall his own features. High cheekbones, short nose, thick head of hair. Is that right? Yes, yes, his fingers confirm it. His skin is cold, like bone itself.

His jaw aches. He's hungry. He dreams of steak and wine, but his stomach constricts and he falls to the snow, heaving.

The rule is, Stay where you are until they find you. Too late for that. But the polestar's clear. He's sure of his direction.

A curtain of color bursts above his head. The aurora borealis. Cepheus, Cassiopeia, Ursa Minor, awash with red and green. An hour or so later the sun begins to rise. Ridges and gullies take the light inside their slowly forming ice, glow from within.

He can see the camp far off, figures running toward him. The whole plain is lighted, like a tungsten bulb. He laughs. Stops to catch his breath. The last stars fade.

Part Seven

DADDY, how do fishes put their coats on?

One fin at a time.

What kind of jacket does a yellowjacket wear?

A jacket made of rice.

What do roly-polies do in the middle of July?

Watch gangster movies in the alley, in the back of the horned toad's home.

What does a peach tree eat, Daddy, that it stays so thin?

Shoe buckles left in the rain.

What does a falling leaf wear?

A lemonade T-shirt.

Who are you when I'm not here? Daddy?

The children's questions get bolder. Does he hate Pamela? What happened to Jill? Was she nicer than Mom? (Jill is very happy with her job at Murray State College and her new live-in, a fellow *est*-ian who once met Albert Einstein.) Adams answers the best he can; he's comfortable with the kids. There even seems to be less tension between Toby and the rest of the world.

"Did you almost die," Toby asks.

"No. If I died, you'd get all my money. I didn't want that to happen."

"I wish I could've gone along."

Deidre stops what she's doing to listen.

"Maybe someday you'll be in a job where you get to go places."

"I can't draw," Toby says.

"You can be a travel agent—"

"A stewardess," Deidre adds.

"Or an interpreter. *Essen*."

"That means 'eat.' "

"Your mom's been teaching you."

"She says the world's going to blow up. Is that true?"

"I don't know. What would you like to eat?"

"Ice cream," Deidre says.

"Besides dessert."

"Mom said you almost died."

"*Peach* ice cream and strawberries and Cool Whip. And french fries with catsup."

"One thing at a time. Burger King? And no, I didn't almost die. Your mother jumps to conclusions."

"I don't think she hates you anymore," Toby says.

"Good."

"Maybe she just doesn't like you very much."

. . .

He moves the silver-framed photograph of Pamela and the kids to a place on his desk where it can't be seen.

At eleven-fifteen he receives an unexpected telephone call from Joseph E. Morgan, senior vice president of Comtex. Morgan sincerely apologizes for Adams' mishap on the ice. If the team had been better equipped, etc. etc. Can Comtex make reparation?

"Well," Adams says. "Essentially it was my fault."

"I'm very impressed with the work you've done for us. I'd like you to know, we're developing our own cartographic staff. Any chance you'd consider us?"

"I don't know," Adams says. "What did you have in mind?"

"I'd like you to interview, of course, but I can give you a general range. . . ." He mentions the low fifties. Adams promises to get back to him.

At lunch Carter is jubilant. "We're continuing to expand, Sam. Since you've been gone we've added two new data bases and increased our statistical and digital capacity." The Deerbridge Road development has been a huge success and Carter has started a new housing district, early American to modern, geodesic domes.

"I've been offered a job," Adams tells him.

"Oh?"

"Comtex wants me."

Carter closes his menu. "Bastards. Goddamn headhunters. Lend you to them for six months, next thing you know—"

"It's a very attractive package."

"How much?"

"It's not just the money. I'd be happier in research and development. You know that."

"I need you on my projects."

"Several of the young guys are ready. Rakofsky, O'Connor, Lajoie."

"They're kids, Sam. I can't even speak their language, much less get a subtle concept over to them. Haven't I given you what you wanted? You wanted an international assignment, I let you go."

"I have no complaints," Adams says. "But when a better offer comes along—"

"What the hell would you do in research and development?"

"Expand our catalog. We can't do fieldwork in deep space, but the computer can take us there. It's an area we haven't touched."

Carter shakes his head. "I'm not sure there's a market for the stars, hmm?"

"Oh, I think there is. Despite its setbacks, the shuttle opened things up."

"You're squeezing me, Sam." Carter picks up the check.

> I try to picture Austin but can only see the dead dry weeds in the field behind my house. It's cold here. I miss you. Irrational, I know, but I keep hoping Jack has changed: self-centered, obnoxious, untidy. I don't know how we'll work it but I'm happy

you want to keep the lines open. I'm used to fixing borders, closing things off.

I can't seem to get moving. The house is strange. Everything's noisy. The refrigerator cutting on and off, the traffic outside . . . it was so quiet on the ice.

When I was little I went into the fields behind my mother's house and listened to empty grain silos howl with the wind that got inside them. Like the sounds of a dying animal. They frightened me. Coming into town tonight, watching the fields rush by, I felt nostalgic about those silos: attempts at order on the prairie.

You once said the academic environment was *it* for you. *It* for me has always been the imagination. I believed we saved ourselves from the size of the world by mapping it, studying it, appropriating it.

Since Svalbard I wonder. *I* was the dying animal out there in the snow, Carol, huddled inside the horse. . . .

He puts down his pen. Perhaps he'll just send her some flowers. Probably she doesn't see many flowers in Texas.

Unless Jack gave her some, had a big bouquet waiting for her when she got home.

He starts to call Kenny; as he lifts the receiver, weariness overtakes him. Too many people, too far away. He places the unfinished letter in the center of his drafting table and, turning off the lamp, goes to bed.

Adams receives an Orb spider and a German

chocolate cake in a ceremony announcing the expansion of On-Line's Research and Development Wing, of which Adams will be the head. For the occasion he has bought a brand-new Brooks Brothers suit, tan, with a white shirt and solid red tie.

Pinning the spider onto Adams' lapel, Carter says, "This man has been a catalyst in our banner year. From local acclaim to international distinction, he's an example of what we all strive to be."

Polite applause from his colleagues. In addition to more money, he's given unrestricted use of a geodesic dome (Fuller's most rigorous design) in Carter's new housing district north of Deerbridge Road. The dome is equipped with a color television, a wet bar, fully stocked, and an IBM PC/XT.

Rakofsky, O'Connor, and Lajoie each receive a bronzed *Ixodes ricinus* in honor of their promotion into Special Projects.

Rosa's been volunteering at the women's shelter and has befriended Pamela. Recently the police asked her if she'd use her power to help them locate a missing baby boy. She closed her eyes, concentrated, and led two officers to an abandoned house, where they found the police commissioner's fifteen-year-old daughter in an erotic embrace with a tractor salesman. "I kept telling them I'm a medium, not a psychic," she says, although she knew before Adams even opened his mouth that he had lost a tooth.

"What else is new?"

"I've become a Black Muslim."

Adams stares at her. "But you're white."

"That's a problem," she admits. "I don't know if the brothers will *officially* accept a white woman, but I'm a brother at heart, that's what counts."

"What brought this on?"

"The spirits told me the balance of world power is going to change very soon. The nation of Islam will rise and smite its enemies, the white supremacists." Her voice intensifies, like a charismatic preacher's. "Ike tried to talk me out of it."

"Ike?"

"Eisenhower. A very conservative spirit. Refuses to admit the cosmic order's shifting. Malcolm told me the malevolent spirits that have manifested themselves in white racism will soon be brought to their knees. And it's not just the United States. You know who's really being victimized in Central America? Blacks, Indians, women."

"Same old story," Adams says.

"You bet it is. Ever hear about *female* political prisoners? No. Women are the poorest people on earth. That's why I joined the shelter. Grass-roots movements are important, but I'm more of an ambassador type. Hell, I've been all over the universe. I've got a broader view than most." She leans back to catch her breath. "The spirits have plans for me."

Adams doesn't know how to respond. Finally Rosa says, "Want to see a movie?"

They go to a *Shaft* double feature at a second-run

theater on the south side of town. Kids cheer as the detective empties his gun into the killer's stomach. There are three other white couples in the audience.

"Isn't he great?" Rosa whispers.

"Yes."

After the movie they drive to Adele's, where Adams orders a sandwich. Rosa wants two poached eggs on toast. "I'm still middle-class in a lot of ways, but I'm working on it. You're going to have to change your maps when the revolution comes."

"I don't mind. As a cartographer, I'm supposed to be objective."

"And as a person?"

"I'm not very political, Rosa."

"*Beyond* politics, that's what I'm talking about, like caring for your kids—how are they, by the way?"

"The most beautiful little people you'll ever meet."

"You don't sound objective to me."

"Let me ask you, Rosa, how've you managed since your husband died. Living alone, I mean."

"I can bring the old fool back anytime I want. I have the gift, remember?"

"Ah."

"You're lonely?"

"A little."

"Well." Rosa spreads her arms. "I make a hell of a spaghetti dinner."

"Pasta won't be banned, comes the revolution?"

"Lord, I hope not." She touches the back of his hand. "You need to have faith in something, Sam. An idea, your fellow workers. When the balance of power changes—"

"Forgive me, Rosa, if I don't hold my breath."

"You and Ike."

Dear Sam,

I'm slow adjusting—seems the cold left an impression on us both. Whenever I hear people talk about work or the goals they've set for themselves, their conversation strikes me as silly. I think of the ice; life here seems awfully easy—and empty—in comparison.

You're the only person I know who understands that.

I've decided to re-enroll at the University of Texas. Ph.D. I suppose I'll teach. I don't know if that will make me happy, but I think, as I said to you, I'll be more comfortable in academia.

Jack is moving into my apartment again next week—can you believe I've let it come to this when I still don't know how I feel about him? Anyway, he's been very nice.

I miss you, Sam. If you'd been here, my decision about Jack would've been much harder. But you're *there*. A place I can't even imagine. And I resent the hell out of you for it. (I don't really mean that.)

Twoo days latrr. I*ve gotten over being angry at you. Forgife the typos but this is Jacks new machine and I've just got contacts. Its like putting bugs in your eyes. Anyway I dont know whatt to say to you Sam but I don't want to quit writing yet. Meeting you was a strange thing in my life. I keep thinking about the last few days, when I hadn't shaved my legs, how delighted you were at the way the light caught the hair on my thighs. You're weird Sam but it turned me on, too. What do I do with you?? I can't picture us together in a n ormal American place. I'd be doing your dishes—it's what youd expect—and that wouldn't work. Still, I'd like to see you on solid ground.

At the bottom of the letter she's drawn a map of Austin, a small rectangle with rounded corners, like a piece of tissue, folded. A blue pencil line labeled *Colorado River* veering down to make the C in her name.

The first thing he does in his capacity as head of R&D is draw a new world map, aided by the latest satellite photography. He studies records of the moon's orbital path, which reveal irregularities in the earth's gravitational tug. The world is pear-shaped, not round, its "stem-end" at the north. Moreover, in the Indian Ocean there is a deep depression. He arranges the information in a computer graphic based on Fuller's Basic-Triangle-Grid, a far less distorted model than Mercator's. Also, using data derived from optical, radio, and laser operations, he maps the earth's gravitational and magnetic fields.

After work, if the night is warm, he heads for the country, to sit at the stone table he has fashioned for himself in a clearing by the dome, light a kerosene lamp, and contemplate his options. Meteors arc slowly across the sky, above the soggy woods, like the boys' rockets in the field behind his house. Often he imagines himself in an enchanted forest, leaves sparkling on the trees, streams winding like trails of smoke through scented shrubs. He is no Thoreau, he thinks. There is nothing mystical about his isolation. He is simply a restless man worried about his work (where does it lead), his desires (how can he satisfy them with the least amount of tension), middle age (is it really the wilderness it appears to be).

Pamela informs him that Otto has smashed up his car in Michigan. He's all right but it's his third DWI. "Daddy's checked him into a sanitarium," she says.

Adams is shocked and sorry.

"I can tell you disapprove. Daddy's just trying to do the right thing."

"The hell he is." He notices a couple of pamphlets on her kitchen table: *Breast Self-Examination* and *Five Facts About Mastectomies*.

She sees him looking at them.

"Don't be alarmed, Sam. I had a mammogram the other day and everything's fine. I just happened to pick those up in the waiting room."

"Just happened to?"

"Well, I *am* a high-risk case. My mother had breast cancer and so did my sister. That means my chances are very high."

"You've never had any lumps?"

"No." She turns on the TV news, very low. The children are getting ready to go with him for the weekend. "You want some coffee?"

"No thanks."

"They're doing preventive surgery nowadays. My doctor asked me to think about it."

"What does it involve?"

"They cut out all the tissue and replace it with silicone. It's called a subcutaneous mastectomy, but that's a little misleading because you don't lose your breast. The whole point is to *keep* your breast."

"You're not considering it?"

"I am."

"That seems pretty drastic, Pam."

"If there's a chance I could lose a breast someday and I can prevent it now, it seems reasonable to me to at least think about it."

"Is this a common practice?"

"It's getting to be."

Adams sits at the kitchen table. "You mean healthy women are going in and having their breasts cut up . . . ?"

"They go in from underneath so the scars don't show."

"That's horrifying."

"I probably won't do it, but it's good to know the option is there. Anyway, I wanted to let you know about Otto in case I have to fly up and help Daddy with the details."

. . .

He used to think it was important to keep up with people. They plan new ways of pleasing themselves or endangering others. Their large mobile homes sweep the land, microwave ovens tingeing the edges of their dinners. They buy new pets and have children, moving on.

Why else would he stand here staring at the lines in the map of his palm? He used to think it was important. He used to think he'd live alone someplace and have severely important talks with himself.

Kenny coughs into the phone.

"Did I wake you?" Adams says.

"No, no . . . just, um. *Sam?* Who is this? Is this Sam?"

"Hey, snap out of it, I'm talking to you."

"Jesus, I just crashed for a second. *Nine* o'clock?"

"Your watch stopped. It's ten out there."

"What are you . . . did I . . . so how are you?"

"Just got back from Pam's."

"*Screw* her."

"No, I don't feel that way. Really."

"Well . . ."

"Just kind of sorry."

"What about?"

"I don't know."

"Tell me about the ice, man. Were you a Popsicle?"

"It was close."

"Dad told me."

"When did you talk to him?"

"Last week. He scared the shit out of me. Said you'd phoned him from London about the trip, and your accident and all. He was really worried."

"I told him I was fine."

"It's not you he's worried about. He gave me the 'old man' routine. He didn't say it, but he thinks I'm too fucked up to look after him when he goes around the bend, and he doesn't know where you're gonna be, running around the world tripping on ice and shit like that. He sent me his CD accounts and his investments. Said he couldn't track you down."

"He knew I'd be home."

"I don't know, man. You figure it."

"He's been like this before."

"He's never sent me his stocks before."

"Well, send them to me. I'll take care of them. Mom still having headaches?"

"Major pain. The migraine that ate Nebraska."

"They're like kids," Adams says.

"Yeah, but it don't bother me. I'm a star now. Video King." His band is called Curveball and they're appearing on MTV in heavy rotation, he says, "wearing leather and abusing chicks. In our next shoot, we're going to desecrate a church. We've picked an old cathedral in Monterey they were going to tear down anyway. It'll be like that haunted house, remember?" When they were little, Kenny and Adams crept into an abandoned house that their friends claimed was haunted. Inside they found the shell of a player piano with a few rusty wires still intact, broken boards, exposed nails in the floor, and cracking plaster. Adams, older than most of the boys, wasn't afraid of ghosts. He tugged on a loose flap of wallpaper and was surprised when part of the wall came with it. The plaster was simply cardboard and chalk, eroded now. He could level this house with his hands. Happily he ran about the room punching holes in the walls. Kenny whooped and joined him. Then, for some reason, Adams felt a presence in the room. He spun around, the heel of his shoe shattering a wedge of glass on the floor, and saw a craggy, vulturous man, hands heavy at his sides. Veins ran like rivers in his temples. Adams trembled at the sight of this horrible ghost; then the man spoke, ordering them out "this very minute." The boys ran, and watched the tall figure from a nearby field. He owned the gas station across the street from the house. Taking a Coke from his machine, he sat out front in a chair near the pumps.

"Anyway, Mom and Dad know I have a steady gig, but they don't know what kind of gig. It might shake them up to see me in leather."

"You're a long way from your roots."

Colored lights circle Morty's eaves like a spangled hem on a Spanish dancer's dress. Inside, a man is stuffing doves into a hatbox. The birds reappear as bouquets.

From the back of the room Adams sees Pete, Denny, and Bob pick up their instruments. The magician performs his final trick. Pete's shaved his head. His shirt says YOU SHOULD HAVE BEEN THERE. The band launches into a Laurie Anderson tune, backed by a Linn drum machine:

> I met this guy, and he looked like he might have been
> a hat check clerk at an ice rink.
> Which, in fact, he turned out to be.
> And I said, Oh boy. Right again.

"They've adapted their style to compete with Bullets," Morty explains. "On the more complicated numbers, Zig sits in with them."

"They're awful."

Morty shrugs, insinuates his hand into Adams'. "Didn't I tell you this was going to be an entertainment capital? Thursdays, we got chipmunks shimmying to a chainsaw. It's a dynamite act. Good to see you again, Sam. Grab yourself a beer on me."

"Things have changed," Bob tells him at the break.

"For the worse, I'd say."

"You don't know the numbers we're doing now."

"It's the same beat over and over. What's to know?"

"Precisely. We don't need to pay a drummer—"

"You sound like shit, Bob."

"I think we sound just fine." He turns to Zig for confirmation.

"Leave me out of this, man." Zig slumps in his chair. "I'm stoned anyway, like on the edge and *falling*."

"I'll audition for you," Adams says.

"You haven't been asked, Sam."

At the next break he rolls out his bass drum and sets it in front of the back curtain, behind the amps. Zig follows with his cymbals. "This is a radical move, man."

"How do you cut the power to this thing?" Adams says, indicating the drum machine. Zig hits a button.

"What are you doing?" Bob yells from the edge of the stage.

"Folks, I'm auditioning for the band," Adams says into a mike. The crowd is indifferent.

He settles himself on the throne, picks up his sticks. Twice as many people in the audience as in the old days. Morty's been hustling.

He hasn't played in six months. His fingers are nimble from his work on the practice pad, but a solo—cold?

He starts with a standard ride on the hi-hat, one-and-a-two-and, one-and-a-two-and, brushing the snare on the offbeat, then rolls into a rumba on the tom. His foot's slow, nothing fancy on the bass.

A rim-shot, a machine-gun roll on the snare, snap 'em to, faster and faster, with hits to the high tom, a little action on the Zildjian, subtle now then loud, make 'em cry, cowbell in the middle of the phrase, slow it down pick it up, building to a run on the snare, faster, louder, draw it out, make 'em suffer, like a long, slow hump, then he's off, rim bass tom high low bass tom high tom bass tom, wrestling with the Dark

Angel. A smoky dirge, the heartbreak blues. A series on the cymbals and he's done. Not quite. Now *then.* The crowd is on its feet.

Pete and Denny take the stage, laughing excitedly. Zig says, "Teach me that?"

Bob picks up his bass. "All right, you son of a bitch," he says with grudging pleasure. "Let's play."

"An old one," Denny says. "It's been a long time."

When they slide into Gerry Mulligan, Miles Davis, Art Farmer, he feels the wings close in around him, the heavy thudding of the angel's many hearts.

Than writes from California:

Things are going well for me here. I just got a raise, and may do some more traveling at the end of the year for Arco. In the meantime I have met a nice young woman who owns a Vietnamese restaurant with her brother in downtown Los Angeles. Nothing serious, but I enjoy spending time with her.

I found your brother's name in the phone book, but so far he has not been home when I have called.

A Soviet scientist I met defected before I left Svalbard. The story I heard says he stowed away on the *Polarstar*, which pulled in beside his mining vessel in Barentsburg. The Norwegians discovered him halfway to Longyearbyen, and he asked for asylum. He seemed to me a very smart man, careful about his work. I'm glad to know he's all right.

I thought of you the other day, Sam. I saw on the news an American military advisor in El Salvador. His goal was to "bring order to Central America." It reminded me of the conversations we had. I hope you'll forgive me, but I can't resist citing one more example of why I distrust the Western passion for reason. At the height of the war in my country, a team of political scientists from Michigan State University arrived to study military tactics, write articles on the special police, and so on. At one time it seemed there were more professors than soldiers in Vietnam. One of the men came up with a blueprint for evacuating villagers. He relocated the entire population of an area into a compound surrounded by a barbed-wire fence. It was like a dormitory, only padlocked and dark. And he dressed the refugees in uniforms—a different color for every village—so he could identify them as he studied their "refugee mentality." He tried to ease the pain of the situation by placing South Vietnamese, rather than American, guards in the compound. But the place was too crowded, too anguished. In time the guards, under stress, began to shoot noisy children.

People they didn't like they kept from the food. I heard of one place where they were chopping each other's hands off—couldn't tell the refugees from the guards. So I don't trust order, I'm afraid. It's not human nature.

Well, forgive me. The news report struck close to home. But it's impossible to dwell on such things when the sun is out and the beach is warm. Come visit. Perhaps your brother could take us to some concerts, and I could reserve a tee-off time at Pebble Beach. Say hi to Carol when you write.

Pamela drops by. The kids want to spend the weekend with some friends. Does he mind not seeing them? He had baked a pumpkin pie and bought three tickets to a basketball game, but he says, "No, it's all right."

She hesitates in his doorway, so he asks her if she'd like a glass of wine and some pie. She accepts.

"I've decided to have the operation," she tells him.

"Oh?"

"My doctor convinced me. And it's not so bad. They can't get all the tissue, but they can get enough to significantly reduce the chances."

"But it's not a hundred percent effective?"

"No."

He dabs whipped cream onto her wedge of pie. "Well, if you've made up your mind."

"I'm scared, Sam."

He sits opposite her with the spoon in his mouth.

"I'm told that for six to twelve weeks after the operation, the sensation in my breasts will be reduced. Some women never get full feeling back in their nipples, but most do."

"Your breasts are lovely, Pam."

She blushes and so does he.

Deidre was a burst of autumn as a baby, red hair, brown eyes, reaching for Pamela's breast, or tumbling on the pink nursery floor, mouth open, waiting for the words to come. Toby, a beautiful mid-winter snowdrift, pale white skin, thick black eyebrows, blessing Adams with beatific smiles and pleasurable grunts. The range of color in a kid as he speeds toward your life and then away, leaving you wordless in the wake of the brilliant violet-to-red rainbow of the Doppler Shift.

Rosa cooks spaghetti Raphael: garlic, a thick tomato sauce, artichoke hearts.

"I talked your wife—"

"Ex-wife."

"Out of having that silly operation."

"Did you?"

"Actually, I shouldn't take credit for it. She decided herself, but I was against it all along. Parmesan?"

"Thanks."

"She's a smart lady. A little naïve, but time'll take care of that."

"She's nearly forty years old, Rosa. If she doesn't know the ropes by now, she never will."

Rosa shakes her head. "She lost fifteen years being married to you."

"Now wait—"

"I'm not criticizing you. But it's true—you both figured it was her job or her desire or whatever to stay home with the clothes. It's the way you were brought up. She has a lot of catching up to do outside the home and she's sharp. Her heart's in the right place. She's committed to art and politics, but she expects too much from them, maybe . . . really thinks she can make a difference overnight, but she'll learn. Already I can see her developing a sense of irony about herself. That's good."

"This Black Muslim kick you're on—isn't that a bit naïve?"

Rosa rolls her noodles with a fork, like a stockbroker reading ticker tape. "You're too young to remember Henry Wallace, but in 1948 he ran for president against Harry Truman. He was vice president under Roosevelt until he got fired, sort of, for opposing the war."

"I've heard Pam's Uncle Otto talk about him."

"Well, he became a one-man party and say what you will about him, I believe to this day if he'd been elected we'd have avoided Korea, Vietnam, the Bay of Pigs—all that crap. I really do. But of course he didn't have a chance—that's what *I* was naïve about. Truman managed to slap the 'communist' label on him, and that buried him. So I been there already. I've had my hopes up. Frank, my late husband, and I flirted with the Communist party for a while but then we heard about the Stalinist purges. We couldn't believe that these people, who we thought were going to guide us in establishing harmonious communities all over the world, could be capable of such horror. So I been to the dance and had my foot stepped on. I got the proper sense of irony about myself, but I've also got the desire to be active still. Pam just doesn't know how hard it is yet—that's her only fault. But she's not the kind to quit. She'll learn, and learn to laugh."

"She quit on me."

"No." Rosa looks at him seriously. "The circumstances changed for both of you. But there was no quitting."

I hope your decision to live with Jack has proved to be a happy one.

I'm lying.

No, not really.

Be smart.

P.S. They found oil on Spitsbergen. We were a good team.

He tapes the card to a rock about the size of a small cat, puts the rock in a box marked FRAGILE. It will cost a fortune to mail, but Carol will be pleased. It is neither pretty nor valuable, just a rock.

"The system is carefully balanced, though operations appear random," Carter says. "It's important for the operations to appear random. People need to believe they have some degree of personal freedom, hmm? Freedom is possible only in a random universe. Therefore, if the integrated nature of the process were revealed, people would rebel and destroy the system. There'd be chaos.

"Don't confuse *me* with the nature of things, Sam. It's bigger than all of us. I'm just a component, like you or anyone else. The man on the street fears technology. He thinks the future's a cloud of waste. I'm saying that the system is self-perpetuating and self-correcting. Minor destruction is inevitable as the system purifies itself, but annihilation is not built into the program. Mistakes condition the future, and I'm telling you the future is preservation."

Adams remembers his last visit with the children. He stopped at an arcade so Toby could play a video game. Screaming men in motorcycle helmets ran around the screen trampling dim figures called phantoms. Sometimes the phantoms ate the arms and legs of the little men, but as long as the head or torso remained, the player continued to function.

Adams spreads his maps out on the table: the world, the earth's crust, the planet's gravitational and magnetic fields. The charts are scientifically accurate and up to date, yet Adams feels something is missing.

Legends are comprehensible. Purposes well defined. Where does the problem lie?

It occurs to him that the world itself is missing from his maps. On one, the planet has been reduced to a photographic reproduction. On another, to a set of numbers. Each new interpretation is an extra inch of kite string, but the string is endless, and the kite, out of sight, keeps tugging beyond his ken.

When Deidre was a baby she learned words quickly: Mommy, Daddy, Toby (which for several months she pronounced simply 'bee). She picked up personal pronouns—he, she, you—but struggled with "me." The last name she learned was her own. Pamela would hold a mirror in front of her chubby face, say "Baby" or "Deidre." She was delighted by her own reflection and dutifully repeated the words, but made no connection with the image until much later.

Most of our words are directed away from us, Adams thinks. Intrigued, he sets out to map the human mind.

For weeks he gathers models, from Aristotle's theory to the latest neurological research. His first thought is to unify the best models with current ideas to form a definitive map. There are so many models, however, each with its own value and charm, that he decides to make a series.

There are mythic models, psychological models, linguistic, philosophical, political, scientific models. Some choices have already been made by virtue of historical significance. One cannot exclude Freud. Existential philosophy should not be ignored. And thinking of Than, he decides to draw a map of the mind according to Hegel.

A Pennsylvania probate court declares Otto incompetent, closes his bank account, and secures his holdings for the present.

"You've stripped him of his civil rights," Adams tells Pamela on the phone.

Pamela, in Pennsylvania, depressed at having to do family business, leaving her latest work to hostile critics (who have grown tired of her *Dangerous Words*), snaps, "You sound like his lawyer."

"I'm concerned about him."

"He's a drunk."

"And Jurgen's a louse for doing this."

"It's been very hard on Daddy. He's not in good health."

"God's punishment."

"Let's not argue about it, all right? Have there been any more reviews?"

Adams had decided not to mention them, but her attitude upsets him and he reads them to her slowly.

To begin with, the base structure of the brain: numerous diagrams exist showing right and left hemispheres, frontal lobe, etc. Problem: how to make a drawing of the brain that isn't just another wiring chart? CAT scans are colorful, but less precise than the best road maps. After long consideration Adams chooses for his Point of View oxygen and glucose, the two most active elements in the brain.

On the computer Adams sketches gentle hills interrupted by valleys, some in shadow, with deep gullies. Dark sky, cobweb stretched across it like a silvery dome. The cobweb represents the arachnoid, a vaulted bridge connecting the crevices of the brain. Cerebrospinal fluid flows like a system of rivers into the valleys, widening into lakes where thoughts splash like noisy children. He gives each lake-child an oversized flashlight, representing electrically charged cells.

Next problem: Is the brain the mind? Centuries of

debate between behaviorists, idealists, dualists, etc., have failed to answer this question.

Constraint (if he agrees that the mind is intangible): a map must refer to a physical landscape.

Whether the mind's assumptions are learned or a priori he cannot show on his map, nor can he determine whether mind is attached to substance and weight.

"He said they were going to take us all somewhere else because we were involved in subversive activities here. This made us very sad because we did not know what subversive activities were."

A Guatemalan peasant. Adams has noticed that the Third World makes up most of Rosa's dead these days, since she has become politically active again. On Tuesday evening Maurice Bishop told her, "In spite of my clash with the CIA, I didn't understand the true meaning of destabilization until I abandoned my body and entered the cosmic realm."

Rosa tightens her grip on his hands.

"Compañeros, Christian greetings from a poor Indian farmer, slain shamelessly on the night of the purge. . . ."

Hegel says there are no bare facts. Things enter into our experience because we conceptualize them. The yard. The barbecue pit. The field behind his house. The boys' rockets. He will never in his life encounter an object he doesn't have words for. Even when something's strange to him, he is able to describe its shape, color, etc.

All things, then, exist as ideas. But every thesis has an antithesis. Every positive a negative.

Negation, Hegel says, is the creative force of the mind.

What does that mean? Adams pauses for a moment. He considers the crescent roll lying on the plate on his kitchen table. My consciousness of that crescent roll depends upon my awareness that I am not a roll. I don't get lost in rollness. Separation (i.e., negation) is fundamental to consciousness.

He wonders how to represent negation on a map, then realizes that maps are by definition negations of territories they do not include.

If every positive implies a negative, it follows that every negative implies another positive, and so on. Self-generation.

The universe is constantly working itself out.

He pours himself another Scotch. The problem remains: *What* is working itself out in the universe?

He picks up Hegel again. "Reason is the substance and energy of the universe."

But where does Reason begin? Like a mathematician, Adams must isolate the principles. The beginning of Reason. It must be the most abstract conceivable thought. *Being* generates *Nothing*, and vice versa, so this, Adams thinks, is the ultimate abstraction: a blank idea into which anything may fit. Being is the quality without which a thing ceases to be itself. He looks at the crescent roll again. He could remove the brown color from it but it would still be a roll. He could change its shape but it would still be a roll. He could take it apart any number of ways but nothing he does can tell him why, when all of the elements are joined, a roll is formed.

Is language Reason? That seems a little suspect. He marks his place in Hegel, buckles his pants, and walks down the block to the library. A white cat zips across the cemetery, a single bulb burns in Rosa's kitchen. Adams whistles a tune as he walks up the street.

In the library he settles himself at a scuffed oak table with several heavy volumes. Locke identifies ideas with all objects of consciousness. Consciousness is the mind's apprehension of its own processes, and the wellspring of knowledge.

But what is an *object* of consciousness? An object, Adams thinks, is something toward which consciousness directs itself. Words? Thoughts? Ideas?

The intentionality of consciousness: It is always conscious *of* something.

Locke is no help.

Berkeley says an idea is a mind-dependent Being. Closer to Hegel, though Hegel would not restrict ideas to the mind.

Sartre: Consciousness is an insatiable hunger.

Adams' stomach growls. He chuckles, catches the

eye of a girl who is trying to study. She gives him a severe look and returns to her book. Adams wonders if he has any cheese and crackers at home. He walks back up the street. The wind rises, blowing paper and cans along the curb. He stops and looks at the field of the dead, the chilly marble stones and bent flowers in copper cups.

What we want, as human beings, is to know.

What we look for in other human beings, a knowing that knows our knowing.

Reason seeking recognition of itself.

The light goes out in Rosa's kitchen. A Volkswagen Rabbit turns the corner, sputtering loudly. Absurd to anticipate Reason in a world that's running down, where people's needs are so opposed. Still, when he recalls Hegel—"Nothing remaining but the mere action of subjectivity itself, the Abstractum of Spirit—*Thought*—" he feels braced.

Hoping is harmless, he thinks. He bounds up Rosa's steps, rings the doorbell. She comes yawning to the door, dressed in men's pajamas. "Sam? What the hell are you doing out so late?"

"Rosa," he says, "Reason is working itself out in the universe."

Adams takes a few days off, leaves the kids with Pamela's friend Cyndi, and flies to Pennsylvania to help Otto adjust after leaving the sanitarium.

"I want to change my will," Otto says. "Cut those

bastards out of it. Pammy's a good girl, but she listens to her daddy."

He's twelve pounds lighter than the last time Adams saw him. A sallow swirl around each eye.

"You don't have anything left to bequeath," Adams reminds him.

"I'll get it back, don't you worry. Got me a Southern lawyer."

That afternoon, while Otto sleeps, Adams talks to the lawyer, a Harvard graduate in her thirties. Her name is Sharon Wells. "I've been hired on a contingency basis," she tells him. "My fee depends on the settlement." She is dressed smartly in a knee-length navy skirt, an Arrow shirt, and a man's red tie. Her hair is ash-blond; round glasses magnify her eyes. "He has a very good chance of regaining his property. They violated his civil rights." She is currently drafting a new will in elementary language, echoing Otto's style, naming Deidre and Toby as beneficiaries, as per his wishes. She intends to videotape the signing in case there is a question about Otto's competency. Adams leaves the office impressed.

He drives his rented car across town to Jurgen's house, a white wooden Tudor, brick trim, picket fence in front. Pamela lets him in. She's thin.

"How are you," he asks.

"Tired." She doesn't seem friendly.

"Your father?"

"Some better. How are the kids?"

"Fine. Cyndi was going to take them to the zoo."

Pamela nods.

Jurgen is also unfriendly. "Why are you helping that old goat?" he croaks, sitting up in bed. Kleenex and bottles of capsules crowd the night table to his right.

"He has nowhere to go. Somebody's got to look after him."

"You think I'd just abandon him?"

Adams shrugs.

"He's my brother, even if we don't get along."

"I'm just lending him a hand, Jurgen."

"Well, it's not Christian charity, Sam, I don't believe that for a minute. You're doing it to spite me."

"I'm doing it because you stuck him in that sanitarium against his will," Adams says, glancing at Pamela. She is standing by a window, letting the sun warm her shoulders.

"Well, aren't we on a high horse?" Jurgen says. "Since when are you so concerned about other people? If you'd worried this much over Pammy, she might still be your wife."

Pamela turns toward the window.

"I think I'd better go," Adams says. "I didn't want to get into this. I just came by to see how you were."

Jurgen coughs loudly and can't stop. Three white hairs wiggle in the middle of his forehead. Pamela pounds his back. Adams brings him a glass of water.

When Jurgen is calm again, Adams squeezes Pamela's wrist, tells her he'll let himself out.

That night, time on his hands, Adams goes to an ice show he'd seen advertised in the paper. Otto is resting comfortably at the sanitarium; Adams' room at the Holiday Inn is too depressing for anything but sleep. The ice show is being staged in a giant arena downtown. His seat is good, a little high perhaps. The arena looks like an airplane hangar, with a green metal roof and heavy rafters. The crowd moves about restlessly on the scarred wooden bleachers. Everyone's wearing a coat.

The show begins at eight. Cold vapors rise from the square of ice, big as a basketball court, on the arena floor. A man dressed as Chaplin's Little Tramp circles the rink, tossing white roses to women in the front row. Adams remembers nights he spent with Jill, the sheen of her legs in the chilly air of her apartment, the warm touch of her hip on his thigh. He thinks of Carol on a bed of snow. He makes a mental note to take Toby and Deidre skating when he gets home, and to buy for them at a hardware store a heavy chain, a fragrant piece of pine wood, a sheet of water-repellent plastic, because these textures are nice to feel.

Otto disappears on the day of the signing. For two hours Adams combs the city. Finally, after lunch,

Otto appears in the lawyer's office, drunk, wearing a checkered flannel shirt. He is covered with hay; he won't say where he's been.

The lawyer tells Adams, "Clean him up. Buy him a suit."

Adams drives Otto to a department store where just this morning, searching the streets, he'd seen a blue serge suit in the window.

"Where the hell do you get off, buying me a suit I don't want?" Otto snaps.

Ties run two for eight dollars. Adams gets a couple for himself.

Back at the office the lawyer signals her assistant to start the videotape machine.

"Are you married?" she begins.

"No, are you?" Otto says.

The lawyer begins again.

Adams tells Otto, "You'll need a place to stay while your case is waiting to go to trial. It could take months. Why don't you come back to Nebraska with me? I've got a place in the country now. It's isolated. You can have it to yourself most of the time."

"Does Pammy know about this place?"

"She never comes out."

"She's awfully upset with me."

"You'll never see her. I promise."

"Sam, my man. What's shakin'?" Pete has let his hair grow back. He's wearing a sleeveless jersey.

"I'm trying to map the universe."

"Heavy," Pete says.

"Do you ever think about it? I mean, do you have a mental picture of what's out there?"

"The universe, man, is a single sax note blown in the face of God."

To Bob, it's a series of cogs.

To Denny, a case of jewels.

Mary, the teenage girl who flirts with Pete between sets, doesn't know but hopes it's soft and cool, like sand at night. "Maybe they'll teach me in college," she says.

"No, books published one week are obsolete the next," Adams tells her.

"Like music, you mean? Heavy metal was in for a while, then disco, then punk?"

"Sort of, yes."

"Well, shit. What's the point of going if everything I learn's a golden oldie before I even get out of school?"

Otto has settled into the dome, an uneasy alliance with the computer. Adams introduces him to Rosa, hoping they'll hit it off, but Rosa has recently purchased an ammunition belt (dummies) and insists on eating a box of chicken wings she has brought. Otto is leery.

"What makes you love black people so much?" he says.

"It's not a question of love." She licks her fingers.

"It's the wave of the future. Even if the spirits hadn't told me, I'd have seen signs in this world."

"What signs?" Otto says.

"Poetry, music, theater, dance . . . the most vital art is being produced by minorities."

"What's art got to do with it?"

"Art reflects changes in the world. The imagination of the white Anglo-Saxon male has run out of gas. Read their books. They're all depressed."

"Let's eat," Adams says.

"That woman's crazy as hell," Otto tells Adams once Rosa is gone.

"I know."

"Why do you hang around a woman that's crazy as hell?"

"She's kind to the children. Keeps me company."

"Married?"

"Widow."

"Probably talked her husband into the ground. Although . . ." Otto props his feet on Adams' stone table. "She's got a point about the signs. I used to figure out what was happening in the country by looking at the ads we painted. Whatever ails you, that's what we put on our billboards. When I first started painting, it was just stomach disorders and colds, then it was female troubles and I knew if that's what people were reading signs about they were talking a whole lot more about screwing than they used to. I coulda told you there was going to be a sexual revolution years before it happened. You just got to watch what's ailing folks."

The tips of weeds in the field behind his yard sparkle like spurs. Bright quarter-moon. Wooden roofs on nearby houses resemble rough thatch.

The man in Adams' yard crouches by the fence, elbow on leg, free palm to the ground. The same man who appeared in the yard months ago. Quickly, Adams slips past the front door, circles the house, and approaches the man, stealthily, from the rear. A light mist is falling. He lifts the latch on the gate. The stranger has not moved. Adams steps forward, not too close. "Can I help you?" he says.

The man turns, keeping his face in shadow. He pushes away but trips over Adams' right foot. Together the men fall in a bed of wet leaves. The stranger tries to rise, slips again. Adams holds his shoulders.

They get to their feet. Adams crouches, ready to tackle. The man is not tall, quick, or imposing. His shoulders are small and smooth beneath the padded suit.

"Pam?"

She loosens her hair and it falls around her face. "Yes."

"All along . . ." he asks, astonished. They haven't spoken since returning, on separate flights, from Pennsylvania.

"Yes." She is breathing heavily, brushing wet leaves from her arm.

After thirty seconds he recovers his voice. "Are you crazy?"

"Of course."

She's mocking him, answering every question in the affirmative. He changes his approach. "Will you tell me what you're doing?"

"Yes." She smiles, loosens her tie, but says nothing.

Adams turns to look at his house, the kitchen light, the drawn curtains.

"Oh no no no." Pamela laughs. "Not a voyeur, Sam. You know me better than that." She removes her heavy coat. "I'm the Man of the Year, the nuclear threat, a lead pipe, a piston. I'm the Terror of the Prairie, the thundering hooves of unperceived radio waves."

She's not drunk. Her eyes are clear and sober. She's putting him on for reasons he can't imagine.

"Okay," he says quietly. "Is the performance over? What the hell have you been doing out here?"

"That's right," she says. "It's a performance, Sam." She rolls up her sleeves. "How long did we live in this house together?"

"Seven years," he says.

"And married for fifteen?"

"Do you want to come inside? Can we talk about this like we're not two crazy people?"

"I like it out here. Country of my Fathers. I am

Zorah, protectress of the men with no heart." She laughs.

"Cut it out. What are you doing?"

"I'm making you uncomfortable?"

"You're acting like an idiot."

"Remember, Sam, art is imitation. The first time you saw me out here, you thought I was a burglar or a pervert, didn't you?"

"I thought you were a guy I knew at work. I didn't know what to think."

"Street theater's risky. If you stage a holdup on a sidewalk, people'll call the police unless you signal them it's all an act. Art telegraphs its intentions. When it doesn't, it ceases to be art. Or ceases to be perceived as art, which amounts to the same thing. Why didn't you call the police on me?"

"I tried. It's not their jurisdiction."

She's greatly amused by that.

"Is that what you call this? Street theater?"

"The Song of the Lorelei, the Poisoned Lozenge, the Terrible Awakening of the Lycanthrope, his wolflike skin, the wrenching echo of his cry across flat country. I must say you disappointed me, Sam. We had one good chase, but that's all."

He looks at her as though he's not seeing her.

"You know the best thing about this house?" she says, absently wrapping the red tie around her hand. "The floor space between the built-in shelves in the living room. Too large to ignore but too small for furniture. You could fill them with wastebaskets, but who needs six wastebaskets in a living room?"

"Come inside, Pam. I'll make you some coffee."

"I used to imagine Alan was sitting in one of those spaces—I swept them every day—or lying on a shelf watching TV with us in the evenings. I never wanted a dead child, Sam. It's hard to know what to do with them." Mist collects in her hair.

"We have two living children," Adams says. "Where are they?"

"Playing with friends."

He rubs the moisture from his face. "You scared the hell out of me. Didn't you think about that?"

"How old would Alan be?"

"I don't know. Fourteen, I think. Come inside."

"I don't live here anymore."

"I'm inviting you in. Will you stop this silly game?"

"I know you won't understand this, Sam, but standing here has given me a wealth of knowledge about the differences between art and life. Moholy-Nagy, Man Ray's *Monument to de Sade*, Florence Henri's *Self-Portrait*, the formal creation of stillness through stable structures—"

"Will you come inside?"

"This is important. Jung speaks of container and contained in marital relationships; conversely, in art, the image and the frame—"

"Then get out of my yard."

"But I am the Hook and the Eye, Collar Bone Stew—"

"Let's get the kids. Where are they?"

"Mother of Hope Unborn."

Dear Sam,

Austin is beautiful in the summer. Mimosa and crepe myrtle. Honeysuckle and roses. The Colorado River is full and near-naked students lounge around the drag in front of the university.

Come see it.

Jack is in California in June, visiting his folks. I can't promise you anything but I *do* want to see you. Any chance?

Let me know. Use the univ. address. Got to run.

Love,
Carol

P.S. You got my map?

It is now late April. Adams and Otto are sitting at Adams' stone table, north of Deerbridge Road. Early evening. The roof of the dome glistens in the sun.

"Pam and the kids are coming out here on Sunday," Adams says. "I thought we'd have a picnic."

"You want me to disappear for a while?"

"No. She wants to see you."

"You're kidding."

"She's making a real effort to be fair."

"Well, I'll be damned." Otto sips his beer. "In that case, can I invite someone?"

"Sure."

"What if I give ol' Rosa a call? She's a crazy old woman," he's quick to add, "but you got to admit, she keeps the conversation hopping."

"She does that."

"Just to break the ice, you know, in case Pammy's got a bug up her ass."

"I understand."

"She won't be wearing a suit, will she?"

"She hasn't mentioned that. Our conversations have been very standard, making plans for the kids."

"Still got a thing for you?"

"I don't know," Adams says. "No. The years we spent together, maybe."

Otto tosses his bottle into a pile of dirt at the foot of the dome. "Can you draw me some kind of map that shows how funny this country is? I mean, even the smart ones like you and Pammy are crazy."

Adams nods. "It's a failure, isn't it?"

"What?"

"The country."

"I don't know nothin' about that."

"Gloriously full. Poisoned, fat, and hungry. A history of odd loves, spurious fights. Rooms that emit high piercing noises just behind the walls. For the next sixty seconds. This is only a test."

"Where do you get all this stuff? Like that shit you were trying to tell me the other night. About Reason?"

"It's working itself out in the universe."

Otto pulls another beer from the Styrofoam cooler beneath the table. "It ain't got a snowball's chance in hell," he tells Adams.

Adams says, "We'll see."

About the Author

TRACY DAUGHERTY was born and raised in Midland, Texas, and educated at Southern Methodist University in Dallas and at the University of Houston. He currently teaches creative writing at Oregon State University in Corvallis, Oregon.